## PRAISE FOR MAILBOAT: BOOK ONE

*I have just devoured an entire bag of pretzels while chewing my nails gripping the end of my couch ... My heart is racing!*

~ Lynda Fergus, author of the Lake House Lyn blog

*Well, if it hadn't been so good, I would have been able to put it down. ... You have me sucked in.*

~ Rebecca Paciorek, reader

*The book far exceeded my expectations ...*

~ Carol D. Westover, reader

*I don't collect autographs, but...zoweee!!!.. send me yours! I was riveted. You have the ability to get inside your characters' heads very well. ... A word of advice: Don't rush out book 2. Perfect it as you did this one.*

~ Sanda Putnam, reader

A HEARTH & HOMICIDE MYSTERY

Danielle Lincoln Hanna

# MAILBOAT

- book one -

A HEARTH & HOMICIDE MYSTERY

Danielle Lincoln Hanna

# MAILBOAT

- book one -

## JOIN MY NEWSLETTER!

- Be the *first* to know about all my new releases
- Access *exclusive* discounts, freebies, and contests
- Get *way* behind the scenes
- Even *help me* write my next book!

Just visit me at
www.DanielleLincolnHanna.com/newsletter

## PROLOGUE

There were no sunrises on earth so damn heart-wrenching as those over Geneva Lake.

Will Read shifted from one foot to the other on the end of the Fontana municipal pier. It had rained last night and the puddles stretching across the white-painted boards splashed on his black Oxfords as he paced. Grinding his teeth and pacing relieved the twisting sensation in his gut—a little. He pulled his hand out of his pocket, letting the hem of his suit jacket fall, and checked his watch for the twentieth time.

Five-o-two A.M. Only two minutes late. But every second dragged like an hour. He shouldn't be lingering like this. He should be on the road for Chicago and his plane for L.A. He couldn't get out of town a moment too soon. Even though it wrenched his heart to leave. He was never going to see a Geneva Lake sunrise again.

The deep rose hues of the rising sun broke through the air like stained glass and scattered its shards over the water. The lake was as calm as the stone floor of a cathedral, broken only now and again by a soft *glugging* as a small wave like a child at prayer washed against the boats in the bay. The air was spiced with the incense of millions of good, clean raindrops, lingering from the night before. Will breathed deep, tilting his head back and

1

closing his eyes. Peace, like a hymn, finally found him, if only for a moment.

He imagined bringing Angelica and the boys here. Showing them the places he'd known as a child. Bringing them back every summer, like his parents had done. Carrying on the tradition.

He flinched and forced the daydream aside. Geneva Lake was dead to him.

He'd laid it on the altar and sacrificed it himself.

A hum broke the morning silence as a lone power boat pushed up a dimple on the surface of the lake. The boat grew larger until Will could make out a bald-headed man behind the wheel, his tanned face as empty and expressionless as a bishop. He maneuvered the boat next to the pier.

Will drew a deep breath and stepped in, offering his driver a nod of greeting, which wasn't returned. Instead, the man pulled back from the pier and pointed the craft's nose toward the east end of the lake, into the sunrise.

Will already knew that any attempt at conversation with this man would result in a monotoned yes or no. So he simply settled back for a silent trip across the length of the lake. Silence was better anyway. He could drink in the wooded shoreline one last time.

The manicured lawns and tree groves slowly passed his view. Pristine white piers. Million-dollar mansions. Pricey weekend getaways for business magnates from Chicago. He'd spent his boyhood summers in one of these. He'd run through it barefoot and sandy-toed. That's what you did if you had money and lived on Geneva Lake. You just ran around barefoot and sandy-toed. A for sale sign caught his eye. He sized the house up and guessed its value. He could buy one of these homes.

Except that his life as a free man depended on never being seen in this place again.

The City of Lake Geneva appeared on the horizon, marked by the historic Riviera. Will choked up at the sight. It was the centerpiece of the town—a castle-like structure sporting two shades of brown brick and arched breezeways under square corner towers. The pitched roof covered an elegant ballroom, built in the Swing Era, and the ground level was full of little shops vending beach food and souvenirs. When was the last time he'd bought an ice cream cone there? He couldn't remember. He had an urge to buy one now.

The boat's driver veered to the right—the south shore—and slowed as the Markham estate came into view through the trees. Will couldn't help his smile. His best friend had lived here, so many years ago. They'd run barefoot and sandy-toed together through the halls. Never mind the halls were marble.

A man stood on the end of the pier with his feet planted and his arms crossed. A good six two, he was muscled like an ox. He wore a silver-studded black leather vest over a white shirt with the sleeves ripped off, revealing brawny arms covered in tattoos.

Such a creature standing on the border of the Markham estate was so incongruous, it set Will on edge. He glanced at his companion for an explanation but couldn't find a shadow of change in the man's face. Instead, the imperturbable driver maintained a steady course for the pier.

The stranger on the pier watched the boat come in and dropped his arms to his sides, flexing his right fist once.

Will turned to the driver. "New gardener?"

He didn't even acknowledge the question.

An acrid concoction of anger and fear mixed in Will's stomach. "Who is that man?"

The driver rotated his head slowly. Looked him in the eye. He paused a beat before a stiff smile cracked the corners of his mouth. Perhaps the expression was meant to be reassuring.

"New gardener," he said.

Something wasn't right. The last time Will had felt this way was when he and his two nearest friends had broken into a bank and triggered a barrage of police gunfire.

Cold reality hit him and sucked the air out of his lungs. This was a trap.

He scanned the leather-clad hit man. Saw the butt of the gun protruding from his belt, not quite concealed under the open vest. If he could get past that brute. Up the pier. Get on the Lake Shore Path. He could run to a neighbor's house. Roust them out of bed. Get them to call—

Call the police?

He'd figure that part out later.

The driver shifted the boat into reverse to slow down as they came within bumping distance of the pier. Tattoos still hadn't pulled his gun. There was a chance, if Will played like he didn't know the man's intentions.

Will rose from his seat casually; even smiled and nodded at the "gardener."

"Morning."

Tattoos nodded back. "Mornin'." He spoke with a thick Chicago accent. He flexed his hand again.

Will stepped onto the pier, watching Tattoos out of the corner of his eye. Should he make a break for it now?

Like a flash, Tattoos went for his gun. Aimed it at Will's head.

Point blank range.

Will jerked to the side just as the bullet went off. It echoed back and forth across the lake, sucking him back in time to the fireworks displays of his youth. *BOOM ... Boom ... boom ... boom ... boom ...*

Will grabbed the barrel of the gun in one hand. Chopped Tattoos' wrist with the other. Twisted, forcing the gun back on its owner. Funny. The man who was now chief of police had taught Will and his friends this maneuver when they were boys.

The way Will held the man's wrist had to hurt like heck. The way the gun was pointed back on its owner had to be scarier than heck. The man's mouth fell open and his hand loosened. Will slid it out of his grip.

And dropped it.

It hit the pier with a thud.

Will thought he heard Bobby and Jason laughing at him. Wade telling him, *That's all right, son. Try again.*

But there was no trying again this time. This time was real.

Tattoos threw him a punch to the gut. Will doubled and staggered backward. With a roar, Tattoos grabbed him by the shoulders and threw his weight against him, forcing him off balance.

Will side stepped, hoping to let the man's own force carry him down. For an instant, it seemed like it would work. Will saw himself running for the path.

A fist grabbed a handful of his shirt. Will's foot snagged in a coil of rope. Suddenly, they were both going down. They splashed into the lake together. Will held ferociously to the lungful of air he'd managed to grab. His nemesis thrashed aimlessly in the water like a slow, fat dog. This was Will's chance to get away. He squirmed toward the surface.

A popping sensation broke through his skin in his left side. Shooting pain forced bubbles of air out of his mouth. With a queasy, stinging sensation, he felt a long piece of metal slide back out of his body. Tattoos drew his arm back for another stab.

Will thrust backwards and upwards through the water, dodging the blow. He broke the surface, shook the water out of his eyes, and gasped for air. Where was the ladder? The ladder up the side of the pier. Where was it?

He caught a glimpse of the driver, sitting behind the boat's wheel, twisted in his seat to watch what was happening.

"Help me!" Will yelled.

The man's face remained expressionless.

With a mighty splash, the surface broke behind Will. There was a growl, and a massive weight bore down on his shoulders, plunging him into the lake again. He didn't have enough oxygen to fuel any kind of reaction. The little he had was seeping into the lake along with his blood supply.

This was it. Game over.

*No. You're going home. This guy's going to be the floater.*

Will twisted to face his opponent and grabbed for the weapon as it came in for the kill. It sliced into his fingers as he gripped the blade, but he ignored the pain. He repeated the same maneuver as before, and the man fell prey to the wrenching pain a second time. The knife tumbled out of his grasp.

Will opted to let go of the man and make for the knife as it fell in slow motion. Tattoos reached a hand out to his throat, pinching his jugulars so the blood pounded in his temples.

Will caught the knife in its free fall and swung it towards Tattoos' rib cage.

Tattoos let go and ducked back, curling both his arms in front of his body. The knife connected with something, but not internal organs. Will may have just added a scar to his ink art.

It didn't matter. He was free. Every cell in his body was screaming for oxygen, and the water was swirling red around him. He lunged for the surface.

Something twined around his feet. The rope. The damn rope! He tried to kick it off.

Instead, it yanked back at him, as if he were a fish and it were the line. Next, a hand grabbed his ankle. Then his shin.

Black dots speckled his vision. A vision of lake weed and greenish water and a man with bulging arms and straining neck muscles. A reflex kept demanding that Will breathe, and the pain from the stab wound finally hit full force, nearly paralyzing him.

Will swung the knife, but only ripped the water.

Tattoos maneuvered behind him. Threw a loop of the rope over his head. Yanked him backwards. His back collided with the pier post. The impact was enough to knock the wind out of him and trigger a big, deep breath.

He instantly regretted it.

The rope tightened across his throat. Stiff nylon fibers dug into his neck. Slick algae caressed the back of his head. His jugular veins strained to push blood up into his skull.

Boys' voices echoed through his head. *Fritz! Fritz! Come play with us!*

Fritz?

That was his name once. Many years ago. Fritz, the boy who spent his summers in Lake Geneva. Fritz of the Fourth of July fireworks displays. Fritz of the bare feet and sandy toes.

His windpipe snapped and the lights went out.

# CHAPTER ONE
## BAILEY

So, okay, maybe three miles per hour doesn't sound fast, but when you're hanging off the side of a tour boat, gripping a handful of mail, trying to jump onto a three-foot-wide pier—all of a sudden, three miles per hour is, like, really fast. Then whirling around and flinging yourself at the boat again before it's gone ... I'm just saying, it takes guts.

Which is something I don't have.

So I truly don't know how I turned out to be so good at this whole mail jumping thing. But it totally rocks, and all the kids at school know it. They're jealous. Of me. Bailey Johnson. This is pretty much the only lucky thing that's ever happened in my life. I could have spent my summer flipping burgers. Or peddling souvenirs. But I'm not.

I'm a mail jumper.

Captain Thomlin—Tommy to pretty much everybody on the planet—touched the helm without taking his eyes off the lake. I had a ton of respect for a guy who could steer a two-deck tour boat within three feet of a pier.

"Watch your step out there," he said. "This one gets slick when it's wet, so don't slip."

I bit my lips together, trying really hard not to smile. It had rained last night. I could see for myself the pier was wet. The winter hadn't been so long that I'd forgotten how embarrassing it was to land on your bum.

But that was one of the things I liked about Tommy. Always keeping an eye on the hazards for me. I have no clue how I survived nine months of torture—a.k.a., sophomore year—without him. Like the high-heels fiasco at prom, and a million other embarrassing school newspaper headlines. All those times I spent curled up in a stall in the girl's room, crying my heart out ... for some reason, my thoughts would wander to the Mailboat, and glittering summer days on the lake, and Tommy standing at the helm. I was pretty sure he was the only person in the world who gave a rip about my pathetic life.

Or so I liked to dream.

On the other hand, maybe he just didn't want me to throw off the schedule by missing the boat. He did run a pretty tight ship.

Tommy pulled back on the two levers beside the helm and slowed the boat down. He squinted at the water.

"I don't know how close I can get, Bailey. There's something down there."

I squinted at the upcoming pier. On a calm day, you could make out every frond of lake weed. But last night's rain had stirred up whatever muck secretly hid in its depths, and with scuddy clouds drifting in front of the sun, all I could tell was that something had lost its battle with flotation at the bottom of the nearest pier post.

"In and out?" I asked. On tricky piers, Tommy sometimes nosed in and pulled the boat to a stop instead of cruising past lengthwise. In the grand scheme of things, it was actually harder that way, since stopping a great, big boatful of 150 people was like stopping a herd of charging rhinoceros.

"Nah. We'll make it. But we'll have to let Markham know he's got some sort of debris at the end of his pier."

I swung my other leg out onto the rub board. Tommy says it was custom built extra wide just for the mail jumpers. And I'm like, yeah, right. Eight inches. That's all the space I have to work with. And there I am, hanging on to the handrail, waves rolling off the prow and churning beneath my feet, a skinny little pier coming at me, and spindly posts offering to skewer me if I don't time my jump right.

And P.S., don't drop the mail.

I leaned out as the target came within range. This was going to be a big jump. Tommy was giving a wide berth to that UFO. (Un-floating object.) I scrunched my legs. Tested my grip on the mail. The envelopes were rolled up inside a newspaper like a paper-and-postage-stamp burrito, secured with a rubber band for easy drive-by delivery.

The first pier post swept by. I jumped.

*Bang.* My landing sent a shock wave through my knees, but I hit the dock running. The tourists made little squeaks, as if vocalizing their excitement would guarantee the success of my mission. My gym shoes made their own vocalizations on the wet pier. I went in for a sliding stop to the mailbox and—*whoosh.*

It is *so* embarrassing to land on your bum in front of a boat full of people. Gee. Did Tommy say something about the pier being wet?

The passengers sucked in a collective gasp. I was fine, except for my pride. But every second I sat there, the boat was passing me by. That was the thing. It didn't stop. Not for the mail, not for the mail girl, not for anyone. It just kept going like ...

Like a herd of charging rhinoceros.

I scrambled to my feet. Ripped open the mailbox. Fumbled with incoming and outgoing mail. Hoped I got it right. Slammed the door shut, flipped the flag down, and sprinted like mad for the boat.

It only took me a split second to gauge the length of the pier against the speed of the Mailboat. I was screwed. I knew it. The passengers knew it. They groaned like a hundred and fifty voices wired to one brain. By the frown on his face as he looked back at me, Tommy knew it, too.

My gut sank. I hated messing up his schedule.

I doubled my speed. The pier vibrated beneath my feet. It crashed and splintered behind me like in the adventure movies. Or maybe I just imagined that part. The passengers cheered. Waved me on. Shouted my name.

One guy pointed down at the water. "Oh, my God. Look!"

I shoved the mail between my teeth to free my hands. On the tip of the pier, I lunged—stretched—reached—

The lake was really cold that morning.

## CHAPTER TWO
## TOMMY

Oh, that girl. The surprised squeak and the splash told me the whole story. If the boat had been closer, she probably woulda made it. But I couldn't get any nearer without knowing what that thing was underwater.

That thing.

I'd tried to get a look at it as we went by. I wasn't sure. The sun was ducking in and out behind the clouds. Bailey's splash would give me a chance to circle back and look again.

Ideally, the mail jumpers make it all the way around the lake dry, but it's always kinda fun if they don't. As I turned the boat in a wide circle, I looked back over the passengers. Most of them were laughing over Bailey's mishap—their secondary reaction after minor heart arrhythmias all around. One animated young man on the shore side was gesturing to his group of friends.

"Dude, there was a guy down there. I swear it."

Most of the passengers didn't know it yet. It was better that way. I wanted to keep them calm as long as possible.

I picked up the microphone and thumbed the power switch. My voice filled both decks.

"Looks like we lost our mail girl. There's still a couple of deliveries left, so I'm taking volunteers."

Laughter filled the boat.

## CHAPTER THREE
## BAILEY

Clear water. Clear, bubbly water. Like I'd been dropped into a glass of lime soda. Only it didn't taste like lime soda. It was in my mouth and up my nose and working its way down into my lungs. My feet were tangled in something— long, slimy weeds with evil little minds full of murder. The more I kicked, the tighter they twisted around my ankles and climbed hand-over-hand up my legs. One of them felt more like a nylon rope.

Seriously? Don't litter. This is how whales die.

My blood pounded like a subwoofer from my heart to my fingertips. My head started to turn light and fluffy. Few more seconds, and I could be walking on the water on moonless nights.

I twisted around, grabbing for the twine-y, slimy mess keeping me down, and my hand bumped something soft and swollen.

Another hand, floating limply in the water.

## CHAPTER FOUR
## TOMMY

As I circled back, I watched my own wake quietly splash the pier posts and roll on toward the shore. Where was that girl?

I'd been driving the Mailboat close to fifty years, and in all that time, I couldn't remember having a mail jumper quite like her. She was athletic, she was good at the job, but you could never tell what she was gonna do next. Like stop on a pier to tie her shoe. She made me laugh. And just as often, she made me shake my head and wonder what was going on inside hers.

I like all the kids who work for the company. I don't have "favorites." But I had to admit, Bailey was ...

No, I wasn't going there.

My mind skipped back to another summer, like someone had cut a reel of film and spliced in a scene from another movie. Two police officers knocking on my door, bearing news. About my son. But not because he'd died. No, he was very much alive. I suppose I should have been grateful. But sometimes truth is worse than death.

The result was the same. I never saw my son again.

The passengers were beginning to mutter. It takes about two minutes to turn the boat around. Two minutes.

Within three minutes, most people will lose consciousness underwater. Bailey hadn't surfaced yet.

I picked up the mic again. "Noah, come up here, please." The PA system was the only way to communicate with my crew member working concessions on the aft deck.

A white fleck bobbed on the surface of the water near the pier. Outgoing mail. They got away from us every once in a while. But normally I'd see a mail jumper swimming out to rescue it.

Not this time.

The sight of that forlorn letter ... all of a sudden, my heart skipped a little harder.

## CHAPTER FIVE
## BAILEY

Screaming underwater doesn't work so well. All those times my foster dad tells me to keep my mouth shut? This woulda been a smart time to do that.

"Debris" really wasn't the right word to describe the object submerged at the end of Markham's pier. Actually, he probably would have been quite the hunk, if he hadn't been all dead and everything. You know, tanned skin, sun-bleached hair, bulging biceps. Beach dude in a business suit. But the fact that he was tied to the pier post by his neck—with his head hanging at a weird angle—yeah. He needed to work on his approach if he was trying to pick up chicks.

It didn't help things any to realize that the rope tangled around my ankles was the long end of the same rope securing Beach Hunk to the pier post. It trailed across the bottom of the lake and twisted around a concrete mooring block before reaching up to hold me in its sinister grip.

I was tied to a dead guy.

Did my life flash before my eyes? No, thank God. Reliving the past sixteen years would have been a fate worse than death. Oddly, the loudest thought in my head at that moment wasn't the dead guy—staring at me with bulging eyes and hair rippling in the current like lake weed.

Nah. It was the crushing realization that I was never going to find my real dad.

Yeah, I was kidding myself anyway. The rope now claiming my life was a phenomenal metaphor for my whole existence—kicking against a system that never intended to give me a chance. But a kid could dream. And I had dreamed. A lot. Like, my whole life. Someday, he was gonna come for me. My dad. He wouldn't leave me adrift forever ... would he?

Yeah, but he had. Sixteen. Still in foster care. Life sucks. The moment you realize nobody loves you—it's like, totally lame.

My wet, bubbly world started going black and static-y around the edges. Entire muscle groups I didn't know I had burned like the morning after the first day of mail jumping. All of a sudden, letting go seemed really easy. What did I have to lose? Not much. No one would even miss me. I'd probably be the only person at my funeral.

Just as the lights were blinking out, a dark blue shadow drifted across my underwater sky.

The Mailboat.

Tommy had come back for me. How cool was that?

Well, duh, of course he came back. Didn't he always?

Yeah. Come to think of it. I was statistically more likely than any other mail jumper to miss the boat ... but he had never just left me there.

Pretty neat.

I closed my mouth before any more air bubbles could escape.

Right, so the creepiest thing about this guy I was hanging out with in the weed patch—he had a knife. He was kind of holding it out to me, like he was saying, "Hey, kid, don't end up like me."

I pried the blade out of his hand. He didn't complain. He didn't have a heck of a lot of use for it now anyway. But I don't know. Maybe I did.

17

## CHAPTER SIX
## TOMMY

I slowed the boat as we neared the pier. The last thing I needed to do was get in Bailey's way if she was trying to swim for the surface.

"Get the life ring," I told Noah. "You're gonna have to go in after her."

Noah swept away the clutter on the counter top and flipped it up. What looked like cabinet doors were really a hatch to the cutty in the bow of the boat. Noah's face was set hard. It was a lot to ask of a sixteen-year-old—to rescue a drowning victim who was both his co-worker and his high school classmate. But he had a determined look on his face. I realized I could rely on him.

The Mailboat had been operating on the lake for nearly a hundred years, generation after generation. I'd been working for the company almost half those years. And we'd never had a serious accident. I wasn't going to let that change today.

Not with Bailey.

Noah emerged from the cutty with the life ring, wisely left his cell phone on the counter, and made for the window. I was leaving plenty of space between the boat and the pier to give him room to work in the water.

Without forward motion, the Mailboat was essentially a sixty-ton bobber.

I wasn't close enough to see that thing at the bottom of Markham's pier. Or Bailey.

Any day of the week, a mail jumper was prepared to end up in the lake fully-dressed—but never before to rescue another drowning jumper. If Noah was nervous, he didn't show it. He climbed through the window, pushing his blond bangs out of his eyes as he scanned the lake. He looped the rope in his hand, getting ready to jump.

Suddenly, the water splashed up like a fountain and Bailey surfaced. She gasped for air, then started hacking up mouthfuls of the lake.

The passengers erupted into applause and cheers.

I released the breath I hadn't realized I was holding.

Bailey shook water and a wet pony tail out of her eyes. Still hacking, she glanced around, then made strokes for the ladder up the side of the pier as if she had sharks on her heels. She hauled herself up then knelt on all fours, coughing.

She had a strand of rope knotted around her ankle and something in her fist. I squinted.

A knife?

I put the boat in motion again and aimed to nose in next to the pier on the far side, away from the strange object. Stopping the boat, starting, stopping again—it was a lot to ask of the boat. But I was used to the Mailboat's every move, and the lake's every wind and wave. I gave cursory thought to the helm and the levers, all the while keeping my eyes glued to Bailey.

She took one look at the boat, scrambled to her feet, and threw herself at the railing. Noah reached out to steady her and guide her in.

"You okay?" he asked.

Bailey tumbled through the window, still sputtering and whimpering like a puppy. Was that water running down her face, or tears?

I put the screws in reverse and eased back from the pier. As I went past the strange object, I leaned out the window and stared down into the water. I wasn't the only one. The boat yawed to starboard as several passengers leaned out their windows.

"See! Right there! Right there!"

"Oh, my God!"

I put the boat in forward motion and made straight for the Riviera. "Noah, call 911 and ask for an ambulance for Bailey."

Noah grabbed his cell phone from the counter.

"And the police," I added. "We have a drowning victim."

I was about to pick up the microphone and advise the passengers that the tour was terminating prematurely. But Bailey put a hand on my arm and shook her head.

"He was killed," she said.

## CHAPTER SEVEN
## RYAN

I was thoroughly accustomed to wearing a bullet-proof vest by this point in my career ... but not with cargo shorts. Or a bike helmet. For that matter, I wasn't used to being a reserve officer—cop for a day, or in my case, a summer. But there was no help for that now. As I tried to stroll confidently down the halls of the City of Lake Geneva Police Department, painfully conscious of my Neanderthal legs bared to God and the world, I wondered whether giving up my sergeant stripes in Minneapolis had really been such a smart idea.

Of course it wasn't. Not if career, advancement, and job security meant anything, and to intelligent people it did. Working bicycle patrol in Lake Geneva would be like going back to rookie. All the other kids on two wheels were fresh-faced with the ink still drying on their diplomas and their first oaths of office echoing proudly in their ears. They were working their inaugural jobs as real cops, and going home to their young brides to tell them thrilling war stories about ticketing jaywalkers.

I was the only grown-up in the pony riding school.

And when the summer was over, then what? My position in the Minneapolis PD was gone. I'd just move on to another department.

Again.

I wondered if I'd ever quit making stupid decisions. Why was one set of coordinates on the face of the globe never a long-term stay for me?

I stepped into the large room that doubled as briefing room and break room. No one else was there. I was plenty early enough for a cup of coffee. I set my bike helmet down on the counter and pulled open a cupboard door. I was a veteran at bumbling my way through the layouts of new police stations, large and small. But for once in my life, I didn't have to try six different doors before I found the foam cups.

They were right where they'd always been. It warmed the proverbial cockles of my heart. Many things change in Lake Geneva as frequently as the four seasons—old houses being torn down, the American Dream of the previous resident; new owners laying down a cool couple of million to raze it and put up their own American Dream.

And then there were those little things that never budged an inch. Like the foam cups. I smiled. You know, in some ways, it was good to be home.

Footsteps entered the break room. I glanced over my shoulder as I poured my coffee, half wondering if it might even be a face I knew.

The woman who walked into the room stopped dead and stared back, her face stone-frozen as if she'd seen the devil himself.

I quit pouring the coffee about the same time I splashed it over the rim.

"Ah! Son of a—" I jerked my hand, sloshing coffee across the counter and my uniform. (Black, thank God.) I set the coffee pot down and shook my hand, flinging droplets everywhere. I sucked the rest off with my mouth. Dammit, that was just like a peach-fuzzed junior high move. I peeked at her, hoping she wasn't snarking.

Her dark mahogany hair was pulled back in a pony tail that trailed down her back like a silk ribbon. Dressed in a black polo shirt and tan slacks, the only things that really distinguished her as a cop were the gun and the badge clipped to her belt and the logo on her shoulder. She wasn't snarking. Just staring. Staring like she'd seen the devil.

Me.

While I was taking in the gun and the badge, I let my eyes flicker over her curvy hips. Nope. Ten years hadn't changed her one bit. Wished I could say the same for myself. Salt-and-pepper temples was a good thing, right? At least I actually used the police department gyms. I still looked pretty damn good without a shirt on. Maybe I should rip it off right now to change the subject from the coffee fiasco.

She finally blinked and came to life. "Ryan. What are you doing here?"

I took my hand out of my mouth. "Working."

"I thought you were in Grand Rapids."

"Was." I ripped off a sheet of paper towel from the roll on the wall and soaked up the spilled coffee, then dabbed at my shirt. It occurred to me I should have done it the other way around. "Then I was in Birmingham, Austin, and most recently Minneapolis."

A stiff smile cracked the corner of her mouth. "You never could settle down, could you?"

Was there a barb in her words? A little double meaning, maybe? Good time to change the subject. I reconsidered ripping my shirt off.

"What about you?" I asked. "You were really climbing the ladder in Madison. Uh—not that you're doing bad here, obviously." Detective was one of the most coveted jobs in any department. The pay was better and the hours more regular (theoretically). I'd worked the position myself once, when we were both in Madison.

23

"My mom passed three years ago," she said. "I came back to take care of her before she died."

The way she said *maahm* and *payssed* warmed the cockles of my heart, too. I mean, not that I was thrilled her mom had passed. Okay, I was. But it had been a long time since I'd heard that *Wiscaahnsin ayccent*. Like a softer version of the Chicago lilt. I wondered if mine had worn off any in all my wanderings. I hoped not.

I wadded up the paper towel and threw it away. "Oh. I'm sorry."

"You hated my mom."

Touché. I made a monumental effort to register no reaction on my face. Monica had a brilliant talent for turning anything I said into an argument.

She shook her bangs out of her eyes. "So, why did you come back?"

I shrugged and picked up my coffee again. "Reconnect with my roots."

Monica cocked an eyebrow. "Well." She cast her eyes over my bike patrol uniform, perhaps dwelling a bit longer than necessary on my hairy legs. She gave me a glassy smile. "Have fun with that."

I stared into my coffee as Monica walked out of the room. Right now, I'd give anything to be wearing my sergeant stripes back in Minneapolis.

Hard to imagine I'd been married to that woman.

## CHATPER EIGHT
## BAILEY

I hadn't planned on ending the first tour of the season wrapped up in a white tablecloth, hacking up my lungs, while the whole lower deck gawked at me. I perched on my cracked vinyl swivel stool at the front of the boat and hugged the tablecloth more snugly around my shoulders. My summer was literally starting out like a wet blanket.

Tommy picked up the mic as we approached the pier at the Riviera. "We ask that you stay in your seats while we dock. Once we're tied up, we'll take care of Bailey, after which we'll proceed to unboard. Thank you for your patience."

*We ask that you stay in your seats ...* It dawned on me that I'd always assumed he was using the royal *we* when he said stuff like that, since nobody would really care if *I* asked them to stay in their seats.

Tommy eased the boat in alongside the pier, practically parking it on a pinhead while Noah jumped off and tied the moor lines to the metal brackets.

A policeman in a helmet and cargo shorts stood on the pier next to a black bicycle. It struck me as weird to be riding a bike while wearing a gun. But then, I'd never tried it. And there were a lot of things that would be weird to do while wearing a gun. Like just about anything.

Tommy reminded the passengers to please stay in their seats while "we" took care of Bailey. Then he put a hand on my shoulder and led me to the door.

The policeman stood on the pier with his hands on his gun belt. "You must be the young lady who fell in?"

I nodded.

"There's an ambulance on the way."

"I'm fine. Juss fell in." My teeth chattered and my voice sounded like a toad with a sore throat. Not particularly convincing.

"She was under for quite a while," Tommy said. "She should get looked over."

"The EMT's are right behind me," the policeman assured him. "What's this about a fatality?"

"Back by Markham pier," Tommy said, motioning toward the south shore. "Pier 980. Bailey says it didn't look like an accident."

"What do you mean it didn't look like an accident?" he asked me.

I peeked my mouth above the folds of my tablecloth. "He wazz tied by hizz neck to the pier."

The officer tilted his be-helmeted head. "Say again?" I didn't think it was because my words were slurred.

I pulled back into my turtle shell and shook my head. I didn't *want* to say it again.

"I'm sure it was just an accident," the officer said. "Got tangled in a rope, poor guy."

If he was trying to make me feel better about what happened, it wasn't working. I *knew* what I'd seen. How does a guy in a business suit end up tied to a pier post by his neck?

"Pier 980?" the officer asked.

"Yeah," Tommy confirmed. "It's 980 South Lake Shore Drive from the shore side."

The officer raised his eyebrows. "You're good."

"You get to know the route after a while," Tommy replied with a grin.

The officer turned to me again. "And what's your name?"

"Bailey Johnson," I croaked.

"Okay, Bailey. We'll get you taken care of."

"I'm fine," I said. "Juss fell in. Happens." Come on, mouth, work with me.

Concern flickered across the cop's eyes. "About how long was she under?" he asked Tommy.

"A good two minutes. She got some water in her throat. She's been hacking up a storm."

"Did she pass out?"

"No."

The cop shook his head at me. "Still, you need to get looked at. Just in case the water got into your lungs. The ambulance is here now. They'll take care of you." He pulled out his cell phone. "Why don't you give me your parents' phone number? They can meet you at the ER."

I felt my face flush. "My dad's working. He won't come."

"Of course he will. What's his number?"

I chewed my lip. This guy obviously didn't know my foster dad. I relinquished the phone number anyway since he clearly wasn't going to drop the issue. He'd figure out the rest for himself.

"Thanks," the officer said. "I'll give him a call. And I'll drop by later to ask you about what happened. When your voice is feeling better."

Two guys in white and black ambulance uniforms rolled up the pier with a stretcher. Oh, great. I was going out in style. I told them I could walk just peachy, but they coaxed me onto their instrument of torture. While they were divesting me of my tablecloth to replace it with a warmer blanket, I suddenly realized I was still clutching a knife.

"Oh. Here." I handed it to the cop.

He stared at it. "What's this?"

"Dead guy had it. Probably tried to kill his murderer with it."

## CHAPTER NINE
## RYAN

I rested my hand on the butt of my gun and gawked down at the knife while the EMTs rolled the girl away. It was a tactical knife with a black handle and silver highlights on the grip. The blade was about six inches long and two inches wide and concave at the tip. The brand name embossed on the handle wasn't anything fancy—probably the kind you could pick up at Walmart in the hunting and fishing section—but still. I wouldn't want to get stabbed with that sucker.

I looked up at the captain, Tommy Thomlin. I couldn't believe he was still driving the Mailboat. He'd been around since I was a little kid. Longer, probably. I thought back on the summers that I worked with him as a mail jumper and it felt like yesterday and an eternity at the same time. I'm sure he didn't remember me—unless he remembered my antics, God save me. It had been years. But truly some things never changed. Like my curiosity over whether *Tommy* was his actual first name. Some said it was just a nickname.

"Murderer, Captain?" I asked.

He motioned to the knife. "She says she took that outta his hand. Used it to cut herself free of a rope she got tangled up in. Maybe the victim was doing the exact same thing. Just wasn't as lucky."

"We'll get it looked into." I dug in the bicycle bag on the back of my bike for a plastic evidence bag. Maybe it was something, maybe it was nothing. Most unattended deaths were nothing. But they all had to be investigated as murder—on the off chance it was. "Anything else you can tell me?" I asked as I stowed away the knife.

Tommy shook his head. "That's all I know. Maybe Bailey can tell you more. I've gotta get these people off and turn the boat around for the next tour."

"I'll let you get back to work, then."

"You know where to find me if you need anything." Tommy grinned.

I smiled back. "Are you ever going to retire? Or are you just going to go down with your ship?"

Tommy chuckled. "Good to see you in town again, Ryan." He waved and disappeared into the boat.

I hoisted my eyebrows, surprised. How many mail jumpers must he have seen come and go over the years? I did some quick math and came up with more than a hundred, maybe two. But I didn't exactly look like my teenage self anymore. I grinned as I remembered how interested the man had always been in our lives. He'd been just like a second father to all of us. Which was pretty damn lucky for me, because my own father had been AWOL.

I walked my bike up the pier and under the archways to the brick courtyard in front of the Riviera and stood under the angel fountain. Kids threw coins into the water and couples took selfies. I tuned out the throngs of mulling tourists, pulled out my cell phone, and dialed the number Bailey had given me.

The phone rang four times before someone picked up. "Yeah?" a gruff voice shouted across the line. The background was filled with loud music, clanging ceramic ware, and lots of voices.

"Hello, Mr. Johnson?"

"Who?"

"Is this Mr. Johnson?"

"Wrong number."

The line clicked in my ear. I pulled the phone away and frowned at it. I was sure I'd copied the number Bailey gave me correctly.

Had she given me a fake number?

## CHAPTER TEN
## MONICA

I stepped out of the elevator onto the second floor and marched straight for the administrative suite. I breezed through the receptionist's room, shared by the departmental brass, and rapped loudly on the chief's door.

"Come in."

I shoved my way in. "What is that man doing here?"

Wade Erickson turned from his computer and looked at me over his square-rimmed reading glasses. By the tilt of his narrow head, I could see where the white buzz cut was designed to hide thinning hair on top. The man was almost ten years past retirement age, and still sitting behind that damn desk.

"Who?" he asked.

"You know who."

"Ryan Brandt?"

"Yes." I crossed my arms.

A smile creased the corners of the chief's mouth. He leaned back in his leather chair, which squeaked under two hundred pounds of mostly muscle. Except for a minor bulge on his belly, he was in good shape for a sixty-something. "Is this an official inquiry? Maybe we should go into one of the interrogation rooms so you can run video."

I sighed. I was coming on too strong. As usual. I rotated my shoulders to loosen them up. "How could you not tell me?"

"I had a certain number of positions to fill and a certain number of applicants, of whom Brandt was well qualified. Or am I supposed to run this department on the individual prejudices of my employees?"

"He'll only be here for the summer, right?"

Wade shrugged. "Depends on if I get a permanent opening at the end of the season and if he applies. As I said, he's well-qualified."

"Because if you hire him, I'll quit."

Wade's eyebrows lifted. "Monica, I know you two have a lot of history—"

I held my hand up. "Never mind. I just—I needed you to know how I feel."

He smiled. "You don't usually leave a lot of room for doubt."

Before I could dish out a clever comeback, my phone rang in its clip on my belt.

"Sorry, Chief. I'm back to work." I picked up my phone as I stepped out of the office. Caller ID said it was Mike Schultz, one of the patrol officers. "What's up, Schultz?"

"I think you'll want to come look at this. We've got a DB tied to a pier post. Underwater. We're at 980 South Lake Shore Drive."

What the hell? I backed into the chief's office again and pulled my phone away from my ear. "Unattended death, Chief. Suspicious circumstances." I talked into my phone again as the chief rose from his desk. "I'm on it, Schultz. Thanks." I tapped the screen and tucked the phone back into its clip. "Sounds like the body was disposed of in the lake."

"I'll come with you."

I turned to head out the door for the second time when someone in cargo shorts materialized out of nowhere and

33

blocked my way. I bristled involuntarily. Was I going to keep walking into him all summer?

"Have you been notified of the unattended death?" he asked.

"Yes. We were just on our way."

"I just came by to drop off some evidence."

"Then do so."

"On *your* case."

I put my hands on my hips. "What the hell are you doing with evidence on my case?" I didn't care how many or what kind of positions he'd worked across a dozen departments. Here he was, first day back, in a temporary position, and he was playing detective? In front of the chief? I smiled inwardly. I'd trip this joker up and get him fired.

"The victim was reported by the folks on the Mailboat. The jumper fell in and saw him. She took this off him." He held up a plastic evidence bag with a large tactical knife inside. "I was the responding officer, so she handed it to me."

Damn. I swiped the knife away from him. "Not that I'll be able to get anything off this."

He grinned annoyingly. "I can throw it back in the lake, if you like."

"Shut up, Brandt." I pushed past him. As I did so, I checked my watch so I could date and time the seal on the evidence bag, indicating when it had passed into my hands. "I gotta drop this off in evidence, Chief. I'll meet you by my car in ten."

"Yes, ma'am," Wade replied. There was something jovial in his voice that irritated me. As I walked out of his office, I heard him make an aside to Brandt. "She thinks she's in my office already."

I would be, damn him. And when I was, I wouldn't hire my staff's exes to piss them off.

# CHAPTER ELEVEN
## MONICA

South Lake Shore Drive was an eclectic mix of nice houses parked alongside super nice houses. Sweet little cottages, five-acre estates—they were all thrown together as if no one gave a damn about zoning. But they all had lake access, meaning even the little ones sold for half a million. It was the lake that cost the dough. You'd think it was made of gold.

"Nine eighty," I said. "I know that address."

"The Markham estate," Wade filled in my memory.

Of course. It was one of the historic homes the tourists came to gawk at—an original from the late 19th century. It had been in the Markham family since its founding, if I remembered the info from the boat tours; and I should, since I'd given those tours enough times as a teenager. Mail jumping had been a hell of a summer job when I was in high school and college.

But the dirge-like tone to Wade's voice told me he was thinking about a different, more recent era of Lake Geneva history, and a Markham that would have been about the same age as me—let's just say forty-something—if he'd lived. They called him Bobby. I'd been a patrol officer back then, still in the early stages of my career. But I remembered. Just not as vividly as Wade did.

He looked out his window and took a deep breath. That was his only commentary on what had happened sixteen, seventeen years ago. I couldn't remember the exact date; I was sure Wade couldn't forget it.

Okay, let me just set the record straight. Despite what the media would like people to think, the vast majority of cops work an entire career without ever killing someone. A few aren't that lucky. Wade was one of the unlucky ones.

I nearly sighed, too. We graduated the police academy dreaming of doing a damn of good in the world and maybe saving a few lives. Sometimes the job is cruel to the dream. Like those times when you have to decide who's going home tonight—you or the other guy. Wade or Bobby. I always believed Wade made the right choice.

In the end, I didn't need the address. I was clearly looking for the place with the swarm of emergency vehicles glutting the street in front—police, fire, and EMS. Their sirens were silent but their lights spinning. Neighbors stood around in little bevies, gossiping. A string of yellow police tape spanned the trees on the berm, like a scrawny rookie with a surprisingly big voice, somehow keeping the spectators at bay.

Outside the police perimeter, on the curb, I noted a uniformed officer standing with two older gentlemen, one in a loose gray cardigan and the other in a crisp, blue button-down shirt and matching tie. The officer was Mike Schultz, a ten-year veteran of the force and too good looking with that black mustache. It was a crying shame he was ten years too young for me and married with kids. But I wasn't interested in dating anyway.

The man in the cardigan, I thought, was Roland Markham.

"That's Bobby's father, isn't it?" I asked.

"Yep."

Whatever a millionaire was supposed to look like, this one didn't fit the bill. He'd combed the hair across the top of his balding head, and the cardigan and penny loafers looked like they came from a second-hand shop. He could have been mistaken for hired help, rather than the landed gentry of the sprawling white mansion.

"You two have a history?" I asked.

"Much like you and Brandt. Best friends growing up. Now he hates me."

I rolled my eyes. "Don't say that man's name."

"Sorry."

"Should you really be here?"

"It's my job to be here."

I shrugged. "You're the boss."

I parked behind Schultz's cruiser. Wade and I popped open the doors to my SUV and stepped down. As we walked toward Schultz, I saw that Markham was watching us. If there was any tension, he hid it well. He stood with his hands behind his back and observed us calmly through little wire-rimmed glasses.

He nodded at the chief. "Wade."

Wade rested his hands on his gun belt while making an effort to keep his stance relaxed. "Hello, Roland," he returned. I'd never say he was afraid of anyone—particularly a frail old man like Markham—but neither would I say he was entirely in his element at that moment.

Markham turned to Mike Schultz. "Well, if that'll be all?"

"I'm sure Detective Steele here will want to talk to you later," Schultz replied.

"Of course." He seemed to make a point of addressing Schultz, and not Wade or me. He gestured toward the man in the crisp blue shirt. "I'll just be at my neighbor's house." He and his neighbor turned and walked away without so much as a nod at Wade.

"We've sealed off the entire yard." Schultz held up two empty rolls of police tape. Big yard. "The body's out back," he added, motioning toward the lake.

"Front," I corrected him. The side of a house facing the lake was always considered the front—even though the white, porticoed "back" door visible from the street was nothing to sneeze at.

"Whatever," Schultz replied. "I don't earn enough to live on the lake and have my yards flipped around backwards."

Wade shrugged. "Don't look at me. I just sign the checks."

Nomenclature around here was for asshats. As if front and back yards weren't confusing enough, there was also the technical difference between *Lake Geneva*—the town—and *Geneva Lake*—the body of water. Most people just called them both *Lake Geneva*, and few people knew there was a difference. Unless you'd been born and raised here and had a fourth-grade English teacher who pounded it into your head for some godforsaken reason.

"What are the signs of violence on the victim?" I asked.

"Why don't you look for yourself?"

He produced a clip board with a check-in sheet from under his arm and offered it to the chief first.

Wade held up his hands, as if it were hot. "You know the rules. The fewer feet in there, the better."

All to make my job easier. I appreciated that. "Let me grab my gear and I'll sign in," I said. Back at my SUV, I slung my DSLR camera around my neck, tucked my notebook and pen under my arm, and found a box of shoe covers. When I returned, I stopped to pull a pair of the covers out of the box. "What does the homeowner know?" I asked Schultz.

"He says he was at home all day yesterday and all night, but didn't hear or see anything. He has security cameras, though."

"Excellent." I envisioned wrapping this case up in short order. If the face wasn't already in our records, we could post a clip to Facebook and have our civilian street team ID the culprit for us.

I glanced across the sea of manicured grass as I slipped the plastic footies over my shoes. "Were you wearing these?"

"No. Sorry."

"I'll need to photograph your shoes, then."

I knelt down with my camera and Schultz lifted a foot, holding it by the ankle. I snapped a photo of one shoe, then the other, and made a mental note that I should probably get Markham's penny loafers, too. And the neighbor's, if he'd been on the property.

"Any obvious places where I should watch my step?" I asked as I jotted the photo numbers in my notebook with the tag *Schultz's shoes.*

"The ground's soft from the rain last night. But I didn't notice any footprints."

"And where exactly is the body?"

"At the very end of the pier. In the water. Just look straight down. You can't miss it."

"Got it."

I signed the check-in sheet and wrote beside my name the exact time of day. Schultz initialed it, then I ducked under the yellow tape. I found my way past the sprawling white mansion to the—*front*—yard, which was itself three times the size of my entire lot. Searching this sucker was going to take forever. Thank God a number of our officers were trained as evidence collection technicians.

The yard sloped down to the lake and a white-painted pier where a classic wooden boat and an even more veteran steam-style launch bobbed in the water. The place was dripping with history and money. And Wade had been best friends with Roland Markham growing up? Crap, I wished I were friends with a millionaire.

As I crossed the yard, I kept my eyes sharp for footprints or anything else that could tell me the story of what had happened here. But the grass and the brick walkway, as much as I could see of them, were a blank slate. I made a guess that if anyone had walked here last night, they would have known the soft ground would yield footprints and they would have stayed to the brick path. I walked on the very edge of the path, not wanting to leave confusing dents in the ground, but not wanting to accidentally smear anything that might run down the center of the walkway. But both looked obnoxiously blank.

I crossed the Lake Shore Path—the public hiking trail that circled the entire lake. Someone could easily have entered the premises from this access point. But still no footprints. Maybe whoever had been here had come by boat, leaving no trail for me to follow whatsoever. I'd be dependent on those security cameras, in that case.

I let myself through a white picket gate. The lake was abuzz with patrol boats—one from the Geneva Lake Law Enforcement Agency and another two from the Water Safety Patrol. I exchanged waves with the drivers. They guarded the lake-side perimeter with their lights blinking. Rubber-neckers had congregated here, too, in watercraft of various stripes. Those boaters I ignored.

At the end of the pier, I finally found a pair of footprints, outlined in specks of water. But I checked the two images on my camera's SD card, and they matched Schultz's tread. I photographed them anyway and wrote *Schultz's footprints* in my notebook.

I looked down into the water. The ripples from the mulling patrol boats broke up the image of a blond-headed man, fully dressed in a business suit, apparently standing on the bottom of the lake and leaning against the pier post.

I squinted. "Weird." Schultz was right. He appeared to be tied to the post. A long string of white nylon rope trailed through the water, leading up to his neck.

No one could expect to hide a body this way for long in the crystal water of Geneva Lake. Either the man had died here, or he'd been left on purpose to be found.

I glanced up at the Markham mansion, even more glorious from the front with a two-story columned patio dominating the lakeside view. Intrigue had found the Markhams once before. Was it stalking them again?

## CHAPTER TWELVE
## BAILEY

I guess breathing water is a big deal. I didn't actually feel all that bad. Okay, my throat felt like burnt toast, and I probably wasn't eligible to drive a car. Not that I had a car. I had a permit. But a chest x-ray and a needle in my arm later, I was still stuck at the emergency room in the hospital in Elkhorn. Waiting for test results, they said.

I fell off a pier. If there was any test I needed, it was how to jump off a pier and land on a boat without getting wet.

"Is there anyone we can call?" one of the nurses asked. Her scrubs were covered in pink and purple teddy bears. Her gloves snapped as she pulled them off. She shook a vial of my blood as if it were a glow stick. I was pretty sure my blood wasn't going to glow, though that would have been cool.

I shook my head. "A police officer was going to take care of that." Calling my foster dad.

"Okay. Will your parents be coming?"

"I guess."

Maybe. Or maybe I'd be calling a taxi to come pick me up. I'd actually like it better that way. I really didn't want to bother my foster dad. It was noon rush at the restaurant. He'd be mad.

The nurse told me to sit back and relax, and she'd be right back.

I sighed—lightly, so I wouldn't start coughing again—and closed my eyes. But when I did, a pair of bulging blue eyes stared back at me from a tilted face. I snapped my lids open again. A start pricked across my entire body in a giant wave.

He was dead. It was finally starting to sink in. That guy was dead. Tied to a pier post by his neck. And I had touched him. I'd pulled the knife out of his hand.

I shivered. Why did the EMTs have to take their blanket away? I wanted it back. I wanted to curl up in as many blankets as I could find and feel warm and safe. I grabbed a corner of the flimsy sheet on the emergency room bed and wrapped it around me, but that didn't cut it.

I shook away the picture of the dead man and searched frantically for something happy to fill my mind instead. My thoughts landed on the memory of Tommy's hand on my shoulder as he had guided me through the Mailboat to the gang plank. I closed my eyes and placed my hand on that same shoulder and rocked myself.

*Gentle arms around me. Rocking me. Don't cry, little one. Don't cry. Mama's here. Mama loves you.*

It wasn't a memory so much as a dream. A dream that haunted me day and night like a ghost with boundary issues. Sometimes the arms were my mother's. Sometimes they were my dad's. Sometimes I even dreamed of both my parents holding me at the same time.

But my mom was dead, and I didn't even have a clue who my dad was.

Maybe if Tommy would just wrap me up in both his arms for, like, the rest of the day, or something. Or maybe just the rest of forever. What did it feel like to be hugged, anyway? To feel safe? To feel as if somebody gave a damn about you?

Strange to crave something so bad when you didn't even know what it was.

I sniffed and smudged something wet off my face. Wrapped my arms around myself. Reminded myself to get real. The only arms I'd ever feel around me were my own. I'd have to make them do.

The door whooshed open and I looked up, expecting to see the nurse. Instead, it was the policeman. Minus the bike helmet.

He looked at me and smiled at first, then frowned. "You okay, Bailey?"

I nodded and sat up straighter and tried not to sniffle again. "Just cold."

"Oh, well here." He turned to a cabinet and poked around for a minute before turning up a fuzzy tan blanket. "Try that on for size. You should have told them you were cold." He unfolded the blanket and draped it over my shoulders.

I felt a small pang of jealousy for little girls who had been tucked in by their daddies every night of their childhoods. "Thanks."

The officer grabbed a little black stool on wheels and rolled it next to the bed. He threw his leg over the stool and sat down with his arms folded across the tiny backrest. "My name's Ryan, by the way. So, what did the doctors have to say?"

I shrugged. "I think they're letting me go home. Soon as they're done with tests and stuff."

"No water in your lungs?"

"Nope. I guess the x-rays looked like x-rays are supposed to."

"Good. Water in your lungs could have led to infection or pneumonia. But it sounds like that shouldn't be a problem."

Infection or pneumonia? Just from falling off a pier?

He adjusted his seat. "I stopped in because I couldn't get a hold of your dad. I think I copied your number wrong." He pulled his cell phone out of his shirt pocket. "You want to give it to me again?"

Whatevs. I repeated my foster dad's cell phone number for him.

Ryan frowned at his screen. "Well, that's just funny. That's the number I have. The guy I got on the line said it was the wrong number and hung up on me."

Why did that not surprise me?

"Do you and your dad have different last names?"

"He's my foster dad."

"Oh-h-h! I asked for Mr. Johnson. Well, still, you'd think he'd know what I meant and that this had something to do with you. It can't be the first time he's been called by your last name."

Actually, since people didn't usually ask about me, it probably was. I shrugged. "It's noon rush. He was busy."

"Noon rush?"

"He owns the Geneva Bar and Grill."

The policeman nodded. "I know the place."

Maybe a little too well. He was a cop, after all.

"So, I suppose he's too busy to come pick you up?"

I nodded again. I'd told him that on the Mailboat pier. Pay attention, dude.

"Well, in that case, how about I take you home?"

"Um ..."

"Or do you already have a ride?"

I shook my head.

"Okay. Then I'll take you."

I shrugged. "Doesn't matter."

He frowned. "Are you sure you're okay?"

"I swallowed half the lake."

He tilted his head forward a fraction of an inch. But it somehow felt as if he'd closed all the space between us to stare me full in the face. "So, is this just Bailey when she's sick? Or is this Bailey the way she normally feels?"

I broke off the stare. It made me uncomfortable. I looked at the cupboards instead. I didn't like his question, either. People don't really ask how I feel. Teachers, now and again, I guess. Social workers. It was like they were always trying to crack my shell. Problem was, I didn't want them to. Why should I? Anybody I'd ever cared about had left me, starting with my own parents. If you can't trust your own parents, who can you trust?

"This is just Bailey when she's sick," I lied. "Kinda sucks being in the hospital."

He gave me a little smile. I noticed for the first time that he had smoldering good looks. Thick hair, going gray at the sides. Strong features. Muscles everywhere a muscle should be. The kind of guy who ended up on the front covers of magazines with their shirts off.

Which was the same as saying I hated him.

"You don't mind sitting on my handlebars, do you?" he asked.

"Uh ..."

Ryan laughed. "Just teasing you. There's a patrol car sitting out in the parking lot. Ever been on a ride-along before?"

I shook my head.

"Well, you'll get a quick one as soon as the doctor's done with you."

I nodded. As if everything were fine with me. It wasn't.

I hate cops.

I hate men.

## CHAPTER THIRTEEN
## MONICA

I leaned on my hand, practicing terrible posture at my desk, and stared into my computer screen, watching in morbid fascination as two divers—one wearing the camera mounted to his face mask—swirled around a pale, twist-necked body strapped to a pier post. They carefully photographed the scene from all angles using an underwater camera. The photos were now uploaded to my hard drive and slowly backing up on the department's cloud storage.

He was a handsome devil. And he certainly knew how to dress for his own death. But how had anyone tied him to a pier post beneath the surface? And was that what killed him, or was he merely disposed of there? I wouldn't know until I got the report back from the county medical examiner.

Half a dozen of us—myself, the two other detectives on my squad, and a number of officers trained as evidence collection technicians—had spent all afternoon combing over what felt like a football field. And what had we found?

Nothing. Absolutely nothing. It was the cleanest damn crime scene I'd ever observed. So clean, it squeaked.

I massaged my temples without taking my eyes off the computer screen. The audio was filled with trickling sounds as the divers breathed through their SCUBA gear. Every so often, bubbles floated past the screen, blocking my view.

The knot behind the victim's neck fascinated me. The perpetrator had made two big bunny ears and tied them into a simple square knot. But due to the loops in the rope, it looked more like a giant bow tie. Perhaps it was meant to complete the victim's outfit.

I snarked.

Ryan hated it when I snarked. I think he invented the word's use as a verb just for me.

Why was I thinking about that asshat again? I mentally shoved him into the lake.

The door to my shared office swung open and the long, tall form of the chief walked in. I didn't bother to greet him. After a brief glance, I glued my eyes back to the video. I was feeling snarky.

"Finding anything?" Wade asked.

"Just that this wasn't an accident." I pointed at my screen. "Look at that knot. Could you picture that knot twisting around the victim's neck without human help?"

Wade leaned over my chair. I saw the reflection of his shaking head in my monitor. "No. That was tied on purpose."

"I'm meeting with the ME in an hour to find out what actually killed the poor bastard." I rewound the video and played it again to get another look at the knot.

"Wait, go back," Wade said, touching my arm.

I didn't like people touching my arm, but I did as he asked. I rewound another minute or two. Back to where the divers were recording wide shots of the victim. "What are we looking at?"

The chief didn't answer. I glanced up at him. His thin gray brows were crossed in a quizzical expression.

"Chief?"

"I know who he is."

I glanced between him and the photography of the victim. "Are you kidding me?" When his eyes remained fixed and on the screen, I decided he really meant it. "Who is he?"

"Fritz Geissler."

I raised my eyebrows. "Geissler?"

Wade gave a twist of his head. "Spitting image."

"His driver's license says he's William Joseph Read from Los Angeles."

"I don't care what his driver's license says. That's Fritz Geissler."

"God damn it."

"What?"

"Now I'm going to be up all night doing homework." I pictured myself locked away down in the dry storage room in the basement, combing over twenty-year-old records detailing the life and times of the infamous Bobby Markham and his associates.

I sat back in my chair and visualized the glittering white mansion set back on the hill. The Markham estate, legacy of well-to-do bankers, who had passed their trade and their millions from generation to generation. Bobby Markham had twisted the path of his forebears and used his inside knowledge to break into a dozen banks all over the Chicago-Milwaukee-Madison area. That is, if we'd pegged all the right crimes on him. Him and his accomplices. Of whom Fritz was one.

"This can't be a coincidence," I said.

"What would bring Fritz back here after all these years?" Wade wondered out loud.

His use of the man's first name didn't escape me, and I was reminded of the fact that Wade had known all these people intimately.

I looked at the body on the screen. "Whatever it was, he regrets it now." I turned to the chief again. "Makes you wonder where Jason is, doesn't it?"

Wade nodded. The look on his face was like he'd seen a ghost.

Maybe he had, in a way.

## CHAPTER FOURTEEN
## RYAN

With Bailey in the passenger seat, I steered the patrol car back toward Lake Geneva and the address on the north side of town that she had provided. She didn't offer a word of conversation during the entire fifteen-minute drive. She looked so small, sitting there with her hands clasped in her lap.

I was fully aware she'd lied to me. This was the normal Bailey, not just the sick-and-in-the-hospital Bailey.

Her small face and button features stuck in my mind. I swore she looked familiar. Maybe it was something about her big, brown eyes. Or the deer-in-the-headlights look on her face. Or maybe it was even something about the emergency room itself—and her in it. But if I'd ever met her before, it had to have been years ago, before I'd left Lake Geneva.

"How old are you, Bailey?"

"Sixteen."

"You go to Badger?"

"Mmm-hmm."

"That's where I graduated. You like it there?"

Bailey shrugged. "I guess. Been to a lot of different schools."

I pulled my mouth into a straight line. Foster kids weren't famous for staying in one location for long. Not if they'd been in the system for a while. "That's gotta be tough. Switching between schools."

"It's okay."

Was everything always "okay" with her? It seemed like nothing was ever fantastic or horrible. Just "okay."

"How long have you been in foster care?" I asked.

"Since I was five."

My heart sank. I was used to steeling myself against the world, but that one really cut. This kid had spent her whole life in the system.

"Where are your parents?"

"Mom's dead. Don't know where my dad is." She said it with the same air as a digitally-voiced weather forecaster reporting the daily highs across the viewing area.

"Well, you must be available for adoption, right?"

"I suppose."

"Is your current family fostering to adopt?"

Bailey bit her lips together and shook her head.

"Sweet girl like you, and nobody snapped you up?"

Bailey huffed. "I wasn't available until my mom died when I was twelve. No one wants a twelve-year-old."

Well. I had explored every avenue, looking for something for Bailey to be cheerful about, and all I'd done was remind her of all the ways in which her life was stuck in the gutter. I drummed my finger on the wheel. *Good going, Brandt.*

Bailey pointed. "That's my house."

It was a ranch with a cement stoop and fifties-era mustard yellow siding as wide as a four-lane freeway. No shutters, no trim, and it looked like the lawn was bringing up a nice crop of dandelions.

"This one?" I hoped I was wrong and she had actually pointed to the cute blue house next door with the hanging flower pots.

"Nope. The yellow one."

Dang. It was an okay house, but that was all. Just like everything about Bailey's life. I didn't feel like leaving her here. I forced myself to pull into the driveway and stopped myself just before I could tell her to stay safe.

"You want a real ride-along sometime?" I asked instead. "This one wasn't very long." For some reason, I didn't want this to be the last time I ever saw her. Maybe it was my cop instinct; maybe it was just me being a decent human. But a voice yelled inside my head to not let her drift away like an unmoored boat.

Bailey paused with her hand on the door handle. "Umm ..." She shrugged. "Nah. That's okay."

Maybe that was for the better. I had forgotten I was slated for bike patrol.

"Well, you take care, Bailey. I'll see you around."

"'Kay." Bailey opened the door and got out.

I reversed the patrol car and got back out on the street. Maybe I'd do a little digging at the station later. That girl just looked so familiar. And if she was in foster care, there was a good chance she was there because I'd rubbed shoulders with one or both of her parents a long time ago.

## CHAPTER FIFTEEN
## BAILEY

I hated people who asked too many questions. I hated cops. And I hated men. I hated everything about being stuck in that car with that question-asking, uniform-wearing, muscled specimen of manhood.

I ran to my bedroom, slammed the door, threw myself down on my bed, and cried.

I didn't make any sense, and I knew it. Because at the same time, all I wanted was for someone to give half a damn about me. And apparently the cop did. Why else would he be asking so many questions? But I hated him too much to let him care about me.

I still remembered the night a cop took me away from my mom.

Something squeaked in the end table next to my bed. It was a nasty metal end table painted puke brown with a laminate top that was peeling around the edges. It squeaked again.

I smudged the tears away from my face and pulled open the drawer. A tiny pink nose peeked over the edge, framed in bushy white whiskers. Two huge, black eyes appeared next, along with two big, round ears. Big, relatively speaking. The ears were barely the size of pencil erasers. But they were big compared to the nose.

He tried to climb out of the drawer and contemplated jumping all the way to the braided rug.

"No, Humphrey, you can't jump that far." I scooped him up before he could commit suicide. His fur was silky brown. His left front leg was wrapped in tiny strips of toilet paper. I'd cut them myself and secured them with a bitty piece of tape. He was clearly feeling better and wanted to run around. I set him on my pillow and watched him dash back and forth and sniff at the tufts of pink yarn holding my blue denim quilt together. Apparently, they fascinated him.

He wasn't a pet. He was a rescue.

Sort of.

I'd found him in the back room at Bud's restaurant, where I worked one or two nights a week. Bud had been shoving hefty cans of vegetables onto a shelf and hadn't heard the tiny squeak. I had. When Bud left, I pulled the veggies back down and found Humphrey with his poor little leg all mangled. I rushed him to the emergency room—better known as the employee bathroom—and conducted first aid with half a square of toilet paper. Humphrey spent the rest of my shift in my backpack and never made a peep. He must have known that his life depended on it.

After work, I sneaked him into my room and lined the end table drawer with newspaper. Later, I added an empty toilet paper roll for him to burrow in and a bouncy ball from a vending machine for him to play with. I was working on a tiny gym, made out of Popsicle sticks. It was coming together nicely. I referred to the drawer as the Executive Recovery Suite.

If Bud ever found out, I was dead.

Only one other person besides me knew about Humphrey. I'd told Tommy all about the Great Humphrey Rescue the next morning. I think he was humored, but he listened to every word as I babbled on as if it all really mattered. I think he thought the name Humphrey was dumb—which it was—but the point is, he listened.

I laid my head on the pillow next to Humphrey and stroked his fur while he sniffed the yarn tufts. I hated all men. They scared me. All of them except for one.

Tommy.

# CHAPTER SIXTEEN
## MONICA

A strong cup of coffee in my hand and my leather-clad notebook under my arm, I flicked the lights back on in the detectives' office. My two partners were gone for the night. I was just getting back. The autopsy had been a blast.

I groaned as I spied a CD sitting on my desk. More work? The markered scrawl across the CD identified it as the security video from Roland Markham's house. A sticky note was stuck to the top of it. The handwriting was Neumiller's, one of my fellow detectives. It had only one word.

*Useless.*

Well, that told me a lot. I assumed the video was poor quality and Neumiller had been too lazy to use our editing software to clean it up. Great. One more thing for me to do. I'd let that one lie until tomorrow.

I dropped into my chair and brought my computer out of sleep mode. I had notes from the autopsy to log into the case file.

Elkhorn had been a joy—if you liked watching medical examiners dissecting human remains. I'd seen it done enough times now that the process interested me more than it phased me. I logged into the police database and started adding my notes.

It was official now: homicide. Estimated time of death was between three o'clock and seven o'clock this morning. The man had been stabbed in the abdomen and bore self-defense wounds across the fingers of his left hand.

According to the ME, the man had still been alive when he was tied to the pier post. Livor mortis had discolored his feet and hands—indicating that his blood had pooled there after his heart had stopped beating. He died in a standing position.

What kind of an asshole would tie up a man underwater, still alive?

Probably the same guy who had crushed his windpipe with a mooring rope.

The ME declared the knife wound non-lethal. It was the rope that had killed our man. The simple nylon rope now tucked away in our evidence collection room was the murder weapon.

Twenty-four hours ago, this man had been alive. Probably enjoying his last dinner. Which reminded me, I needed to try to find out where he'd been staying and where exactly he'd partaken of that last dinner. I needed to find out all his moves—when he'd come here. How. Why. Who he really was. I sighed and slouched and added more items to my mental to-do list.

My night was far from over. I was meeting with Roland Markham for an interview in thirty minutes. Schultz had pre-interviewed him, but that was before we'd potentially identified the victim as Fritz Geissler. Now it was imperative I talk to Markham as soon as possible.

Particularly if the surveillance camera footage was "useless."

I sighed and shoved the CD into the tray on my computer. What the hell. I had thirty minutes. I may as well find out what Neumiller was talking about.

I selected the first file and put the playback on four-times speed. Then I leaned back in my chair, nursing my mug of coffee, and watched as the occasional moth zipped past the screen.

Ten minutes in, I was getting massively bored. Neumiller could have at least told me where to look. I gave up. This could wait until tomorrow when Neumiller could tell me which file to look at and where.

My hand was hovering over the mouse when something changed on the screen. A light flashed past, then everything went pitch black.

What on earth?

I stopped the video and dragged the marker back until the picture of the yard appeared again. I set the playback to regular speed this time. The camera was mounted to the— e'hem—*back* of the house, overlooking the circular brick drive, the fountain in the middle, and the wrought-iron gate, which was standing open.

Moths ... Moths ... That same dumb moth ...

Then there it was.

A bright oval of light appeared on the sidewalk beyond the iron fence. It hovered a couple of feet above the ground, then turned and came through the gate.

A more suspicious mind than mine would have cried "paranormal activity." But I knew what this was and groaned.

There went my swift ID of the suspect.

The halo of light approached the video camera. A gloved hand appeared out of the light, holding a spray can. I noted the label had been carefully painted over. I couldn't so much as harvest a brand name.

Like Neumiller said. *Useless.*

Or mostly useless. I now had a time of day. Four forty-six A.M., according to the time stamp in the corner of the screen. That was more specific than the medical examiner's "between four and seven A.M." I also knew that the perpetrator had indeed entered the property from the street.

I clicked on the other files and fast forwarded them to 4:45-ish A.M. In each one, the halo of light proceeded to every security camera and blacked them out with paint. His path followed the brick walkway that circled the house. He'd stayed religiously to firm surfaces and avoided puddles. No wonder I had no footprints.

That dumb halo. Someone had done their homework. I hadn't seen this trick used very often, but it was effective. Someone wishing to block their image from a security camera could simply insert mini infrared LED lights into small holes in a hat, flick a switch, and bam. The cameras would record nothing but a cloud of light over the wearer's face. This guy looked like he'd gone the extra mile and inserted LEDs down the front of his shirt, blocking all but his legs.

Damn, damn, damn. Not only did I have no suspect, I had no video of him killing Fritz Geissler.

*Useless.*

## CHAPTER SEVENTEEN
## MONICA

"Come in, Detective Steele! Come right on in. Can I get you anything to drink? Coffee? Tea?"

*Dinner?* I thought wistfully. "No, thank you, Mr. Markham." Despite the growl in my stomach, it was my personal policy to never accept food or beverages from the public. Some sorry bastard could be trying to poison me, for all I knew. And if anyone ever succeeded, I swore my skeleton would haunt his house for the rest of his natural life.

Digs like this wouldn't be a bad place to haunt, though.

Markham led me across the marble floor of the foyer, so highly polished I could have done my lipstick in the reflection. A compass medallion sat square in the middle, sporting bits of gray and black marble and aqua blue glass. The compass was superimposed over an outline of Geneva Lake. It was a long, narrow, bumpy-looking lake, but in glass tiles, it looked pretty damn good.

Hell, I'd be happy to haunt just the foyer.

I followed Markham through paneled doors into a living room that could have fit half my house. Glass in white panes overlooked the lake, while various-sized ships in bottles lined the mantle of a long, white fireplace. The furnishings were turn-of-the-twentieth-century, with little clawed feet and rows of brass rivets outlining red velvet upholstery.

Markham's neighbor—the man of the stiff blue shirt and tie—stood behind one of the chairs, one hand folded on top of the other. Carefully creased khaki slacks and gleaming patents completed his look. Where Markham looked almost slovenly with his wispy gray hair and his Mister Rogers cardigan, his neighbor looked too starched to be a lake resident. However many millions they had, they typically dressed as if they were ready to launch a boat or play a round of golf at any second—not as if they were heading off to a business function.

"Detective Steele, I never properly introduced you to my neighbor, Charles Hart."

"A pleasure," I said.

Hart nodded. Man of few words, apparently. Maybe I liked him.

Markham motioned to a gathering of furniture before the empty fireplace. "Have a seat, please."

I'd never yet been poisoned by a leather sofa. I took up his offer. The buttoned upholstery was soft from a century of use and smelled of warm, rich animal hide.

Markham took the opposite end of the sofa, but Hart remained standing. If it hadn't been the twenty-first century, the man could have passed for a butler.

"Well, how goes your investigation?" Markham asked, folding his hands over his knee. He had a high, thin voice with just a touch of gravel, as if he'd been a smoker at some point in his life. "I can still hardly believe it. Of all the places to dispose of a body, why at the end of my pier? I'm still in a little shock."

"I'd say it's been a day of discoveries," I replied.

"Oh, that's good! But no arrests yet, I presume?"

"No. Not yet. Mr. Markham, when was the last time you saw Fritz Geissler?" I jumped right into the question and watched his reaction carefully.

He raised his eyebrows in surprise. "Fritz?" He sighed heavily and added an "Oh, my" under his breath. His eyebrows furrowed as if my question pained him. "I can tell you the exact date I last saw Fritz. It was July the 20th, 1997. Seventeen years ago. It was the night before my Bobby was—" He glanced at me. "The night before he died."

I nodded to let him know I knew. His instinct had been to use the words *was killed,* but I represented the force that had killed him.

"He had dinner with Bobby and me and Jason in this very house. The night after that, they broke into a bank right here in town and ... well, you know."

I nodded again.

Markham shrugged. "And no one's seen Fritz or Jason since. They made a clean escape. Well, you know all about that. Why? If you're suggesting Fritz had anything to do with this murder, I have to tell you. That young man didn't have a mean bone in his body. There's an ocean of difference between burglarizing a bank and killing a man."

"That's not exactly it," I replied. "We've potentially identified the victim as ... as Fritz."

Markham's mouth fell open. "Oh my God."

"Did he come here to see you?" I asked.

Markham didn't reply right away. After a beat, he shook his head as if clearing a fog and looked up at me again. "I'm sorry. I'm still processing this. Fritz is ... dead?"

"We have a conflict between a personal identification of the victim and the victim's ID, but there's a strong possibility that this man is Fritz Geissler. The man's been missing for seventeen years, as you say, so there's no surprise if he was using a fake ID."

"Would a second witness be of help? I knew Fritz well, and both his parents have passed."

I raised my eyebrows. "Yes, if you're willing, that would be a great help."

"I suppose it would involve ... seeing him?"

"No. The medical examiner will show you a photo of the victim's face. That's all. It's up to you whether you'd like to ID him."

"I would, Detective. He grew up with my son."

"I'll make arrangements with the medical examiner. Thank you, Mr. Markham."

"It's the least I can do."

"Forgive me for pressing the question—" (I could be downright charming when I needed to be) "—but is there any reason Fritz would have come to see you?"

"If there was, I would have been more surprised than anyone. I can't imagine why he would show his face in Lake Geneva at all, particularly if he was keen on remaining in hiding. Someone would be bound to see him and recognize him."

"He risked a lot to come here. I'm trying to understand why."

Markham shrugged with his thumbs. "I wish I had the answer for you, Detective. Honestly, I'm baffled."

I looked to Hart. "Did you know Fritz?"

"I did," the man replied.

"Do you have any idea why he would have come?"

"No."

Succinctly put. This interview was becoming massively unproductive. I addressed Markham again. "Would he have come to you for help?"

"You mean, could he have expected help from me if he'd asked for it?" The old man's shoulders slouched as he sighed. "I suppose that's the great question I have to ask myself—a moral dilemma, if ever there was one. I knew him since he was a lad. I knew his parents. I was fond of the entire family. What would I have done if Fritz had knocked on my door asking for help?"

He stopped, staring into the empty fireplace. Finally, he spoke.

"It was Fritz and that boy Jason who led my son down the wrong path. It was their influence that ultimately resulted in my son's death." Markham looked up at me and said with a set jaw, "I would have turned him in."

## CHAPTER EIGHTEEN
## ROLAND

Roland closed the weighty, hand-carved door on Detective Steele and turned to face his old friend. Charles's usually mum eyes were suddenly explosive with a frenzied sort of secret agent flare. He uttered a solitary word and apparently expected Roland to understand a full sentence from it.

"Jason."

"What? You mean where is he?" Roland chuckled somberly. "Wouldn't we all like to know?" He moved into the kitchen—fully modernized with stainless steel appliances and a red brick floor for an unexpectedly updated look. His father wouldn't have known what to make of it. His grandfather would have had a separate kitchen house out back. It was a house in its own right now, expanded, with its own lot, and Charles lived in it. "Coffee, Charles?"

His life-long neighbor followed him into the kitchen. His posture was hunched and his gait hesitant. Very unusual for him. He was always a bit starched. "I'm worried."

"Why? Because Fritz is dead?" Roland pulled a pair of mugs down from the rack.

"Yes. Are you armed?"

"What? No."

"Let me loan you a gun."

Roland filled the mugs and set one down on the counter in front of Charles, then tilted his head forward and stared at him over the rims of his glasses. "The day I need a gun, I will acquire a gun. But that is not today. What could possibly happen?"

"Then let me stay with you. Just until we know where Jason is."

Roland laughed as he raised the mug to his mouth. "I think that's highly unnecessary. You live in my back yard."

"Roland." Charles placed a hand on his arm, his touch unspeakably warm and tender. "You know how I'd feel if ..."

Roland stared at him over the top of his mug. Silence lingered awkwardly, as did the hand on Roland's arm. The ticking of the clock above the stove grew unnaturally loud. Yes, Roland was afraid he understood all too well how Charles felt.

Charles's face deepened to crimson. He withdrew his hand without a word and walked out of the house.

Roland sighed and set down his mug. Charles had married and raised children and divorced—and been in love with another throughout.

And after all these years, Roland *still* didn't know what to do about it.

## CHAPTER NINETEEN
## BAILEY

*Slam.*

The bang of the front door jerked me out of a dead sleep and the sound of someone singing at the top of his lungs made sure I stayed that way. I looked at the glowing numbers on the clock on my bed stand. Two fourteen A.M.

I pulled the covers up over my head. *Please don't notice me tonight.*

Heavy footsteps tramped down the hall. My bedroom light flicked on.

"You assshleep?"

"Yes."

"'Kay."

The light went back off. I released the breath I was holding. He tramped back down the hall. A minute later, I heard the fridge door. A can pop open. The TV come to life. Some late-night comedy.

He'd pass out on the sofa and be hung over tomorrow. Then he'd be out of sorts, but at least he'd be sober. I didn't mind him when he was sober.

I tuned out the TV and drifted back toward sleep.

"Bailey!"

My eyes flew open again.

"Bailey!"

I wanted to crawl further under the covers and stay there until daylight. Instead, I threw back the denim quilt and stood on the worn wooden floor that sounded as if it were about to cave into the basement at any moment. I knew better than to keep him waiting. I walked down the hall and peered around the corner into the living room. "Yeah?" I twisted the hem of my tee shirt in my fingers.

Bud sat reclined on the sofa, his feet stretched out on a coffee table littered with old magazines and empty chip bags. The hand holding the beer rested on his paunch, thinly covered by a worn-out tee shirt.

He looked at me with hazy eyes, then patted the space on the sofa next to him. "Come watch TV with me."

I crunched the hem of my tee shirt in my fist. "Um ... I have to work tomorrow."

"Yeah, so do I." He laughed. "God, I was up at four this morning. Or ... yesterday morning, come to think of it. Been a hell of a day." He motioned with a jerk of his head and patted the sofa again. "C'mon, Bailey. Come sit with me."

I eased slowly into the room and toward the couch.

"There's a good girl."

I let myself down onto the sofa beside him. He put his arm around my shoulder and scrunched me close. I sat and said nothing. Watched the raunchy comedy on TV.

But I kept seeing pictures of bulging blue eyes. Blond hair waving in the current. I felt a rope tangled around my feet. Felt my lungs burning for air.

A tear rolled down my cheek before I could stop it. Pretty soon my nose was running, too.

"Whatchu cryin' for?" Bud asked.

"Nothing."

He pulled me closer, until it was too awkward not to lay my head on his shoulder. He rubbed my arm. Leaned down and kissed my forehead. My mouth. Twice.

I hiccupped a sob.

"C'mon, what's the matter?"

"I don't want to tonight, Bud," I whispered.

He grinned, his face right next to mine, his breath smelling like beer. "Oh, sure you do." His other hand circled my back. "You always do. My Bailey's a good girl."

I shook my head, tears flowing down my cheeks. "I don't want to." I put my hands on his chest and tried to push him away.

But he wouldn't budge. He laughed instead. Pulled me tight against his chest. I squirmed, but he just laughed.

"Let me go! I don't want to!"

I kicked and my foot connected with his shin.

He bellowed and backed off. "Damn you!"

His fist made a dive for my face.

## CHAPTER TWENTY
## TOMMY

I woke up thinking about Bailey.

Robb, the owner and manager of the cruise line company, had called last night to let me know she was all right. No ill effects from her near-drowning incident. She was fine and would be back to work this morning.

And still I was worried. Somehow, her accident had given me more of a scare than I would have anticipated.

I shook the thoughts out of my head and went around my small house to open the curtains and let the sunrise in. I walked into my living room last. The old oak floor groaned beneath my feet as I stepped around navy-and-white striped furniture. The walls and the mantle were full of black-and-white photos of generations past and Lake Geneva in its glory days when carriages ruled the streets and steam yachts the water. A fleeting thought suggested it would have been more appropriate for a man of my age to have my walls filled with photos of generations future.

But there were none.

I stepped up to the bow window. The vintage gramophone sat on a pedestal in the center of the floor, the shape of its trumpet outlined against the navy blue drapes behind it. Before touching the curtains, I loaded an antique disk onto the machine and started it up. A distraction would be good this morning. The Dorsey Brothers scratched to life. I soaked in the Charleston-era jazz music, then pulled back the curtains.

Red streaks across the glass leapt out at me. Lettering, crudely done in all caps. It was written backwards, from my perspective. CLEANING HOUSE. Large drops had rolled down and dried, giving the effect of dripping blood. The skull and crossbones underneath seemed to be there to clarify the meaning.

I opened my front door and looked out at my porch and yard, as if expecting to find some clue. Or even the perpetrator himself. But there was nothing.

*Cleaning house.* What was that even supposed to mean?

I went back in and scrounged up a sponge and bucket. Some kids had nothing better to do with their summers than paint other people's windows. I briefly considered reporting it. But I knew Wade and his crew already had plenty on their plate with yesterday's murder victim. If the vandalism happened twice, then I'd bring it up.

I filled the bucket with soapy water and wiped a sponge-full across the lettering. It dissolved far more easily than I anticipated, running down the window in brownish rivulets. What kind of paint was this?

Underneath the smell of sudsy water, I picked up another, metal-like scent. I leaned closer to the window and sniffed.

Blood?

## CHAPTER TWENTY-ONE
## MONICA

I focused my camera on the dripping red words and clicked a photo. *Cleaning House.* Paired with a skull and cross bones. The meaning was too clear and downright chilling. There was one dead body already.

Roland Markham had been right to call me.

The elderly millionaire stood placidly beside me, his hands in the pockets of his cardigan. Navy blue today. He studied the words painted on his window.

"'Cleaning house,'" he read out loud. "What's that supposed to mean?"

I bit my lip. This was classic of the people in my home town. They saw no evil, heard no evil, spoke no evil. Even if a dead body turned up under their noses.

"You didn't hear or see anyone, Mr. Markham?"

He smiled and pointed to his ear. "I don't hear a thing when my hearing aids are out."

"And your security cameras?"

"The maintenance man hasn't been out yet."

I sighed and mentally rolled my eyes. Didn't this man understand that murder had been done here? "Do you have someplace else you can stay?"

Markham's mouth popped open.

I motioned to the white wicker chairs on his veranda. We each took a seat and I leaned on my knees. "I'm taking this very seriously. Whoever killed Fritz Geissler is clearly indicating a deep interest in you, as well. He left Fritz's body at your pier. He left a message on your window. I don't want to frighten you, but I think you should take some precautions."

"But what on earth have I got to do with Fritz?"

"You knew him well."

"A long time ago."

"And you knew his friends."

"So did a lot of people."

"Roland, those boys practically grew up in this house. Someone might think you know more than you actually do—and they're cleaning house."

Roland twirled his thumbs. Then looked at me over the rims of his glasses. "You mean Jason? The last member of ... of *the ring*." He sounded uncomfortable talking about his son's organization.

"I don't have any names yet."

"He's the only one who could want to clean house."

"He's a person of interest."

"*A* person of interest? Who are the rest?"

I didn't reply. I didn't have any other leads, and he knew it. With Bobby and Fritz both dead, Jason was indeed the last member of the ring.

Roland sighed and patted the arms of his chair. "I just can't imagine him doing any of this."

"That's because you still picture him as a little boy. You *know* he killed a cop seventeen years ago—during the shootout after their last burglary."

Roland grinned and waved a finger at her. "He hasn't stood trial for that yet."

I smiled. True. But if he ever did, the jury would make short work of him. Lake Geneva had lost one of its own, and Wade was still around to testify that it was Jason's bullet that had killed his partner. "Whoever is behind this, I just want you to stay safe."

Roland waved his hand. "Very well, very well."

"So get those security cameras fixed. Lock your doors. Call me if you see anything remotely out of place."

"I will, Monica."

That was the best I was going to get out of him. I hoped it would be enough.

## CHAPTER TWENTY-TWO
## TOMMY

I never did call Wade about the vandalism. Even if the words had been drawn in blood, the message didn't make any sense. I didn't find any deceased animals in my yard. So I cleaned up the mess and went to work.

Bailey came up the pier with her backpack just as I was reeling out the diesel line to fill the tank. Like me, she was always ten minutes early. I like getting a jump start on my day. I didn't know what her reason was. I'd never known a sixteen-year-old who loved getting up early.

"Mornin', Bailey," I called.

"Mornin'." She said it with her head hanging.

I dragged the fuel line up the pier, the hose slithering along the wooden boards. "Doctor give you a clean bill of health?"

"Yep." She glanced at me and smiled before ducking her head again and stepping inside the Mailboat. But in the brief moment that I glimpsed her face, I saw a glaring black eye.

I stopped outside the door and stared at her. "Bailey, what happened to your eye?"

She turned around slowly, her lips bit together. "Um ... I guess I hit something."

It looked like she had tried to tone it down with makeup, but there was no hiding the swollen black circle.

"Hit something? What do you mean hit something? Looks more like something hit you."

Whatever color was left in her face drained away.

I frowned. "Bailey, who hit you?"

She shook her head. "No! I mean ... I think I hit something when I fell in. You know. Yesterday."

I pieced together the scenario. As far as I could tell, there was nothing to hit but open water. "Did you hit the boat?"

"Yeah."

I chuckled and shook my head. "You're not gonna grab the railing with your eye."

She smiled. "Yeah. Pretty dumb."

"Did you have the doctor look at that?"

"Um ... it didn't show up until later."

"Well, still, it must have hurt."

She shook her head. "Not until later."

"You feel headachey or nauseated?" A head-on collision with the Mailboat could create deeper damage than a black eye. Concussion. Fractured bone.

"Nope. I'm fine."

"You up for mail jumping?"

"I'm fine. It's just a little tender."

I smiled. "Well, I imagine it would be." I hauled on the fuel line, creating a large loop of slack. "Stop in the office when it's open and tell Robb about that."

Her mouth fell open. "It's not a big deal."

"Well, it is. It happened on the Mailboat. You need to file an accident report."

Bailey stood there with her mouth gaping.

I removed the fuel cap by the front window, inserted the nozzle, and locked the lever in the open position. Diesel began pumping into the tank. I rubbed the grime from the hose off my hands and turned to Bailey. "Or is it okay to lie to me, but not to Robb?"

Bailey didn't speak. Didn't move. Just stared at me with her mouth open.

I stepped back up to the door and leaned on the pier post. "Bailey, who's bullying you?"

She shook her head woodenly. "No one."

"You don't have to protect them. The only way to make it stop is to tell someone who can help."

She shook her head again, but her eyes were glassy with tears. "No one's bullying me."

"You really got that by jumping at the Mailboat?"

She nodded.

"Are you going to fill out an accident report?"

She hesitated. Then nodded again.

"Okay. Make sure you do."

"Yes, sir."

"That's 'Yes, sir, Captain' to you." I grinned.

A smile finally broke across her face.

"'Kay. Go clean those windows."

Bailey turned away and I went back down the pier for the fresh water line. I didn't believe she got that black eye from her accident any more than I believed the earth was flat. Why would she protect whoever did it to her? She was so timid all the time. Just the sort of girl who could get trapped in an abusive situation. The thought of somebody mistreating her made my blood boil.

At eight o'clock, Bailey set out for the post office to pick up the day's mail. It was only a three-block jaunt, but she'd be gone for an hour, sorting envelopes and magazines. I watched her back for a moment as she retreated, then climbed the short stairs to the aft deck where Noah was stocking the snack bar. I knew he and Bailey were in the same class at the high school, though I wasn't sure how well they knew each other outside of that and the cruise line.

"Does Bailey have a boyfriend?" I asked. It came out more pointedly than I'd intended, but there was no pulling it back now.

Noah looked up, surprise on his face. I guess it was unusual for me to ask about the kids' personal lives. There was a day and a time when I would have known everything about my mail jumpers—but that was before Noah had even been born.

"I doubt it," he said. "She keeps to herself a lot."

"What? Doesn't she hang out with the other kids?"

Noah shook his head. "A lot of them tease her because she's in foster care."

Foster care? How had I not known that? "What happened to her parents?"

"Dead, I think. I don't know. That's just what I heard at school."

"Know anything about her foster family?"

Noah pulled a face and shook his head. "She doesn't talk. I guess her foster dad is the guy who runs the Geneva Bar and Grill."

The Geneva Bar and Grill. I didn't know that much about the place—or the man who owned it.

"That was quite the shiner Bailey got, wasn't it?" Noah asked.

I nodded. "Yeah, it was." And I wasn't going to be satisfied until I knew who had given it to her.

## CHAPTER TWENTY-THREE
## TOMMY

I finished my second and last tour of the day that afternoon and joined the stream of foot traffic outside the Riviera. As usual, every available parking space, paid or unpaid, had been occupied by ten in the morning and once you got it, you kept it. If you planned on going anywhere in this town on a summer afternoon, you were going by foot. Of course, I got downtown so early in the morning, I could have had my pick of the parking. But I didn't live far away, and I swore the daily walk kept me young.

But I wasn't heading home today. Not yet.

The building that housed both the police headquarters and city hall was only a few blocks away. I walked past the flags snapping jauntily in the breeze—the City of Lake Geneva, the State of Wisconsin, and the good ol' Stars and Stripes.

Two sets of double doors led to a space with a high ceiling and stately paintings of Lake Geneva in bye-gone days, when millionaires arrived from Chicago by train and ladies carried parasols over leg-o-mutton sleeves. I took the stairs to the second floor. The balcony was hung from one end to the other with works by local artists, arranged in chronological order. My path led me down the hallway where artists of the late 19th century were represented. No better place to keep these treasures than right outside the office of the chief of police.

I entered the administrative suite and exchanged greetings with the secretary. Wade's door stood open. I knocked on the frame. "You busy?"

Wade glanced away from his computer and looked at me over his reading glasses. I remembered just how old I was when I realized that the man I'd always counted as my kid brother couldn't see a screen in front of his face.

"Hell, yeah, I'm busy. No thanks to you, Tommy, and that cadaver you found yesterday."

"Just trying to keep your nose out of trouble."

"Not in my line of work."

"I can give you a call tonight."

"Nah." Wade peeled off his glasses, leaned on his desk, and rubbed his face like he'd like nothing better than to go to sleep. "I was gonna talk to you anyway."

"Oh? What about?"

Wade looked at me out of the tops of his eyes. "Close that door and have a seat."

I frowned. This was sounding pretty serious. I swung the door shut and lowered myself into the chair in front of his desk.

"You first," he said. "What brings you to the City of Lake Geneva Police Department today?"

"Who owns the Geneva Bar and Grill?"

Wade laughed mirthlessly. "Sad I know the name of every bartender in town. Bud Weber. Why?"

"What do you know about him?"

"We've had the odd call at his bar now and again. Nothing out of the ordinary."

"I don't suppose you know whether or not he does foster care?"

Wade chewed on that before replying. "I really couldn't picture him as a foster parent."

I told him about Bailey's black eye. "I'm sure she was lying. Then one of the other kids told me he thought this Bud Weber person was her foster dad."

Wade picked up a pen. "What's the girl's name again?"

"Bailey Johnson."

Wade talked while he wrote. "And she's the one who found our cadaver?"

"Yes."

"Busy girl." Wade threw down his pen. "What makes you think it was Bud Weber?"

"Well, she doesn't have a boyfriend. They say she keeps to herself mostly. Who else could it be?"

"A bully from school, perhaps," Wade pointed out.

"Could be," I agreed.

Wade tapped his notepad. "We'll check this out. Find out the story behind that black eye."

"Thanks, Wade. I appreciate it."

"Any time, Tommy. I'll keep you informed."

I leaned back in my chair. "Now what's your news?"

"That body your mail girl found. We haven't released his name because we're working on notifying the next of kin. The driver's license in his wallet said he was William Read from Los Angeles. But either that ID's fake, or he's twin brother to somebody I know."

"Who?"

Wade paused and took a deep breath. "Fritz Geissler."

The name hit me like a hammer. A ghost from the past flew in front of my face. I beat it back down inside its box.

"What was he doing here?" I asked, my voice unexpectedly going hoarse.

"Well, that's what I'm trying to figure out."

His body had been submerged off the end of Roland Markham's pier. "Roland," I said out loud. "That can't be a coincidence."

"We've considered the possibility he was after Roland for some reason." Wade shrugged. "But this William Read

82

person doesn't have anything worse on his record than a couple of traffic tickets. And whatever brought him here, the question still stands: Who killed him? Roland doesn't know anything."

"How did Fritz die?" I asked.

Wade eyed me gravely. "It's an open investigation, Tommy."

I nodded. There were some things he couldn't share. Not even about a man I'd once known. A man who was now dead, his body dumped in the lake.

I thought back on the days when I used to run around town barefoot, a bat and glove slung over my shoulder and an ice cream cone from the drug store dripping in my hand. Gone were the days. And now myself and the two boys I used to hang out with—Wade and Roland—were old men, tied together by a shared tragedy from seventeen years ago that had now come back to haunt us.

Bobby was Roland's son. Wade had killed him. And Jason ...

Jason was my son. Or he had been.

"You, uh ... Jason hasn't tried to contact you, has he?" Wade asked.

I shook my head. "You know you'd be the first to know if he had."

Wade nodded. The glasses came off again and clattered to the desk. He rubbed the bridge of his nose. "I don't know where this investigation is going to go, Tommy. I thought ..." His voice trailed off.

"You thought I should be prepared."

Wade nodded. "Tommy, Roland found a message painted on his window this morning. 'Cleaning house,' it said."

A shiver raced up my spine. I didn't say anything yet. Let Wade finish.

"Bobby is dead. Fritz is dead. So. Who do we have left who would want to clean house?"

It was a rhetorical question, but I answered it anyway, my voice barely audible. "Jason."

Wade nodded. Slowly. Deliberately. Studying my face. Watching for any show of emotion, no doubt.

"'Cleaning house,'" I repeated. "I had the same message painted on my window this morning."

Wade sat up. "What?"

"I washed it off already."

He frowned at me. I'd just broken the first rule of police investigations: don't touch the evidence. "Did you photograph it?" he asked.

"No. I didn't know what it meant. I thought it was just kids with nothing better to do."

Wade bit his lip and tapped his pen. There went the second rule: photograph the scene.

I shook my head. This didn't make sense. Roland and I had known nothing about the burglaries. Still knew nothing, besides what had already become public knowledge. Neither of us had known that our own sons had turned thieves in the night.

The spliced reel flashed across my mind again. Police detectives knocking on my door. Letting me know that Wade had just been involved in a shootout. Against Bobby, Fritz, and ...

And Jason.

A police officer was dead. Jason was wanted for the killing. They wanted to know if Jason was with me.

No, he wasn't.

And I never saw him again.

I rubbed my palms on my khaki shorts. "I want you to know this, Wade. If you find him ... if you find Jason ..."

Wade nodded.

"Don't go easy on him for my sake. As far as I'm concerned, I never had a son."

Wade maintained eye contact with me for a moment, then broke it off to twirl the pen on his desk. "You did your best by him, Tommy. He made his own choices. You don't have to keep beating yourself up."

"That's easy for you to say. Your son's an Air Force pilot. Mine's a fugitive. I still run into people who ask me, 'So what's Jason up to these days?' How am I supposed to tell them I don't know because he skipped town seventeen years ago after he murdered a police officer?"

Wade nodded. "I know, Tommy."

"No. You don't. You haven't had to live with this."

Wade's eyes flashed. "Do you think I enjoyed killing Bobby? My best friend's son? We've all had our own burdens to bear. And they're still with us. Every day."

I turned my head and looked out the window. "If you do find Jason … just give him everything he deserves."

Wade sighed. "I don't have any other choice."

## CHAPTER TWENTY-FOUR
## RYAN

When you sign up for the job, you have visions of chasing down villains in fast patrol cars, duking it out in gun battles, and generally living the life of an action adventure movie. No one tells you that you'll spend half your time with your butt in a plastic chair in a room that looks like a school computer lab, writing down every little detail that just happened on the street—even if it's just a traffic violation.

That's what I was doing when the chief and Monica walked in. Recording a traffic violation for all posterity.

"You have got to be kidding me, Wade. I've got to get home and pack. My plane leaves out of Milwaukee in three hours."

"Oh, that soon?"

"I told you that an hour ago."

"I'm sorry. I forgot. I thought you could sneak this in."

Monica folded her arms. "No dice. I'm working a homicide, Chief. So are your other detectives, in case you hadn't noticed. Hate to say it, but your foster care abuse case has to wait a couple days, at least. There's only so much we're humanly capable of doing."

I quit pretending like I wasn't eavesdropping and looked over the top of my monitor. "Foster care abuse case?"

The chief glanced over at me. "Yeah. Remember the mail jumper who discovered our DB? The Mailboat captain is concerned she's being abused."

"On what grounds?"

"She showed up at work with a black eye this morning. Says she got it when she fell in yesterday."

I frowned. "She didn't have any bruises yesterday. I gave her a lift from the ER when I couldn't contact her foster dad. She was fine."

Wade lifted his eyebrows. "Maybe there's something to this report, then."

"Agreed," Monica said, "but when are we going to investigate it? Neumiller is still interviewing the neighbors and Lehmann is digging up every lead we can find on Jason Thomlin. Plus we have the rest of our caseloads."

The chief looked at me again. "Brandt, why don't you take it?"

Monica's mouth dropped open ever-so-slightly. I enjoyed the surprise on her face—and not just because she looked sexy with questioning eyes and parted lips.

Where had that come from?

I shook the wayward thought out of my head. "Me, sir?"

Monica recovered. "Really, Chief? A seasonal patrol officer?"

"I can think of three good reasons why Brandt should handle this case," the chief replied. "First, as you're aware, Detective Steele, there's nothing unusual about me assigning simple cases to patrol officers when the detective bureau is swamped."

I wasn't flattered by the epithet "simple."

Monica threw her hand in the air. "Yes, but—"

"Second, Brandt already knows the alleged victim, which gives him some rapport with her. Right, Ryan?"

Rapport? I thought about yesterday's car ride of silence. "Well ..."

"Finally, Brandt may be a seasonal patrol officer right now, but he has five years of experience as a detective, which is more than I can say for any of my other patrol officers."

I nodded my head sideways. True.

Monica gave Wade an unmistakable stare of death—chin tilted down, eyes burning. "Whatever. It's none of my concern."

"I'm glad for your resounding approval. That's settled, then. I'll get you Bailey's contact information, Brandt."

"I already have it, sir."

He beamed and nodded knowingly to Monica. "You see what I mean." Grinning, he walked out of the room.

Monica's stare of death hadn't abated any. Now she turned it on me. "Congrats, dick."

I knew she meant it both ways.

She turned to walk out.

"Hey, Monica?"

She kept walking.

"Monica!"

She stopped and gave me a bored-out-of-her-wits expression.

"Would you let me into the dry storage room?"

She rolled her eyes. "Why?"

"I need to look up some history on Bailey."

"She's in our records?"

"I think so."

"And this will help your case?"

"Yes." Was that a lie? Maybe, maybe not. Any information could prove potentially useful ...

"What'd she do, knock over a bank when she was three?"

The dry storage room was for older records—a.k.a., ancient history, recorded on cuneiform tablets before the dawn of electronic storage systems. When I'd started my career, I'd written my reports by hand. Much had changed. Except the plastic chairs. The plastic chairs hadn't changed.

I shrugged. Truth be told, I wanted to know only one thing. Sixteen-year-old Bailey was haunting my thoughts. I could swear I knew a far younger version of that face. A face that had grown more mature, but hadn't lost the big, baby eyes or child-like quality. Was I only imagining things?

"I need to know if she's who I think she is."

Monica bounced her eyebrows. She stared me down for a minute, then checked her watch. According to the house rules, anyone who wanted access to the dry storage room had to be kept company by a key holder.

"I'll give you fifteen minutes," she said.

"Well, that's generous of you," I said—considering I only had a vague idea where to begin looking.

## CHAPTER TWENTY-FIVE
## RYAN

Monica unlocked the door to the dry storage room and pushed it open. "There you go, Detective Brandt," she said with a mock bow.

I ignored the snub and walked in, hitting the light. The basement room held a noticeable chill. Gray cardboard boxes on rows of metal shelves contained countless thousands of records—the heartbreaks of an entire city, going back in some cases for decades. I pitied the poor fool whose job it was to clear away outdated documents. The one I was looking for might not even be here anymore.

I sighed. Where to start?

Monica closed the door, folded her arms, and leaned against a shelf. "So, why are we really here, Brandt?"

"I'm looking for information that bears on this child abuse case." I picked a box at random—1999. How old would Bailey have been in 1999?

"No, you're not," Monica countered. "You forget, I know you. I know that look you get in your eye when something becomes personal. This is personal. So what is it?"

I released my breath and pulled out another box. "I guess I'm just trying to figure out whether we actually do any good sometimes." Two thousand three? That was more like it.

"Is that why you keep moving between departments?" Monica asked. "Hoping the crime will be better someplace else?" She snarked.

I flipped through February and March reports. Perhaps it had happened in the summer ... "Maybe," I said. "I don't know. I just get restless, I guess."

I withdrew another box from 2003 and flipped through the documents. My eye landed on one labeled 03-8985. The year 2003, the 8,985th call for service. The date was July 1st. The writing was my own. I pulled the report out of the box. Started reading. Long-lost events came back to life.

A domestic disturbance. The neighbors had called. By the time I got there, a man was waving a gun and threatening to kill his girlfriend. Backup. Hostage situation. SWAT. Negotiators. No shots fired. No one hurt. We talked him out and jumped on him with handcuffs. He was stoned. So was his girlfriend. She had pills in her pocket. She was under arrest, too. We found marijuana, cocaine, and drug paraphernalia littered all over the living room.

And a five-year-old girl hiding in an upstairs closet.

I closed my eyes as the memories came clearer. I'd pulled back the closet door and found her just sitting there. Curly brown hair. Button features. Bruises on her face and arms. I picked her up. Carried her outside to the ambulance waiting beyond the police perimeter. Big, brown eyes. A deer-in-the-headlights expression. No tears. Just a soulless stare.

According to the report, her name was Bailey Johnson.

This was her. I'd handed her over to the system myself the night I'd picked her up off that closet floor. And she was still in foster care. Still a ward of the county. Still had no idea what it was like to have a home and family of her own. I felt hairline cracks spreading across every surface of my heart.

"So. Tell me, Ryan." There was a hard edge to Monica's voice. "How many women have you slept with since we broke up?"

I winced. I was already feeling low about myself on account of Bailey and my role in her misery. I didn't need Monica dredging up my past failures right now.

I fanned the edges of the reports in the box. The old Ryan would have evaded the question. Made excuses to justify his behavior. Played the truth down. I still hadn't nailed who the new Ryan was—other than that he wasn't supposed to run anymore.

I turned around and looked Monica in the eye. "Seven." Not counting one-night stands. Okay, maybe I was still evading.

She bounced her eyebrows. "Impressive. And how many women are you going out with right now?"

"None."

"The female population finally figured you out, did they? Good for them. We may be slow, but we're not stupid."

I smoothed the papers with my hand while I tried to keep a lid on my mouth. One thing was obvious: I wasn't going to ask Wade for any permanent position, like I'd planned. I might not even stay the summer. In fact, I'd start sending out my resumé to other departments tonight.

But a voice inside my head piped up. *Quit running away, Brandt.* That same voice told me that everything happened for a reason. And maybe Monica was the reason I'd come back to Lake Geneva.

I closed my eyes briefly. Oh, this was gonna kill me.

I looked at my ex-wife again. "Monica, did I ever tell you I was sorry?"

She chewed her lip and studied a corner of the ceiling dramatically. She shook her head. "Nope. Can't say you ever did."

"Okay then. Monica, I cheated on you. I'm not proud of it. I realize now that I really hurt you. I'm sorry." I spit it all out before I could think of turning back. And I looked her in the eye with every word.

Monica stared at me blankly for several excruciating moments. Finally, she laughed and cracked a mirthless smile. "Sure, Brandt." Spinning on her heel, she marched out of the dry storage room. "Time's up."

I sighed and shoved Bailey's report back into its box. Well. I'd come here to reconnect with my roots.

## CHAPTER TWENTY-SIX
## MONICA

Ryan's apology meant nothing to me. Empty words. That's all he ever had been. The empty vows he'd uttered on our wedding day still echoed in my ears and burned a hole in my chest. I wouldn't trust him with a dog I didn't like.

Eight hours afterwards, I was in Los Angeles, relieved to be half the country away from Mr. Ryan Brandt, if only for a day and a half. First thing in the morning, I was behind the wheel of a rental car, following my GPS app onto a secluded, palm tree-lined street.

Wade and I had debated long and hard about the costs that would be incurred with sending me all the way to Los Angeles. But it wasn't every day we encountered a case of this magnitude. Fritz Geissler had taken part in siphoning millions of dollars out of banks throughout the Chicago-Milwaukee-Madison area. And now he was dead. And his last living cohort, Jason Thomlin, was still at large.

I pulled up in front of a pair of ornate but heavily-secured gates blocking the street. Leaning out my window, I buzzed the number for the William Read house.

"Yes?" a female voice hummed over the speaker.

"Mrs. Read? This is Detective Steele."

"Oh. Come in."

The gate buzzed and slid open. I put the car in gear again and drove forward.

Scanning street numbers, I watched porticoed houses with four-stall garages march past my windshield. It was Lake Geneva, minus the lake. I was kind of curious to get a peek inside one of these mansions, but I wasn't particularly looking forward to this interview. It was going to be complicated. Local police had already informed Angelica Read of her husband's death. Now I was here to dig up his dirt.

Well, whatever he'd been up to the past seventeen years, it was paying good.

I found the house number on a Mediterranean-style villa with red clay roof tiles. Once I'd parked in the wide driveway, I grabbed my portfolio and stepped out. Flagstone steps led to a porch decked in arches and hanging flowerpots. I rang the bell. A deep tone vibrated through the house.

The door swung open and a small Hispanic woman with free-flowing hair and dark eyes stood inside. She was barefoot in white shorts and a breezy, sleeveless yellow top. Her eyes were damp. She'd been crying.

"Hello, Mrs. Read. Detective Steele."

The woman accepted my handshake. "Please come in." She stretched the *i* out into a long *e*.

I stepped over a bamboo rug with boys' shoes in two different sizes neatly lined up along the edges. Angelica led me down a couple of steps into a living room with a flying ceiling. A wall of glass overlooked a back patio and a lush, jungle-like yard.

"I'm very sorry for your loss," I said as I settled into a white satin chair and set my portfolio on the glass coffee table.

Angelica sat on the matching sofa and tucked up her legs beneath her. She leaned on her elbow on the armrest.

"There's been some mistake, Detective. My husband was never in Wisconsin."

The statement hit me between the eyes. "I'm sorry?"

"Will went to a convention in Las Vegas. He was nowhere near Lake Geneva."

"Where is he now?"

"Las Vegas," she said simply.

I shifted in my seat. One part of my brain insisted there was a huge misunderstanding. Another part of my brain scrambled how to explain to Wade that I'd just wasted hundreds of dollars of departmental funds. "You've spoken with your husband?" I asked.

"I've called him. There must be something wrong with his cell phone. It sends me straight to voicemail. I've left messages for him."

Oh, Lord. The truth finally struck me. The woman was in denial. She was frantically trying to contact her husband. Calling a phone that had spent hours under the surface of Geneva Lake. My eyes darted to the glass end table at Angelica's elbow. Her cell sat there, alongside a box of tissues. She was waiting for him to return her calls. Dammit. I had no choice but to break this woman's thread of hope. I knew her husband was dead.

But the question of the day was whether Angelica Read knew all of her husband's secrets—and whether I could get her to reveal them.

"What does your husband do, Mrs. Read?"

"He manages the Central Bank of Los Angeles. He's been in the financial industry for many years."

As had Fritz Geissler. He and Bobby and Jason had all worked for Roland Markham's firm out of Chicago. Then they'd taken what they knew of bank security and used that knowledge to devious ends. Frankly, I was stunned Read stayed in the same industry. What the hell had he told prospective employers?

"Where is your husband from?"

"Michigan."

Smart man. That was close enough to his real home state that it might very well be familiar to him—in case associates and acquaintances ever asked questions. "He has family there, I suppose?" I suggested. "Parents? Siblings?"

"His parents are in Grand Rapids."

That had to be a lie. My research on Fritz Geissler said he was born and raised in Chicago, spending summers in Lake Geneva. On top of that, his parents were now dead. "You visit them, I suppose?" I asked.

"No. Will doesn't speak with his parents."

Aha. In other words, they didn't actually live in Grand Rapids. His entire backstory was a fabrication. But did his wife know that? "Who is Fritz Geissler?" I asked, throwing it out at random. I liked throwing questions out at random. Just to watch my interviewee's reaction. Subconscious facial expressions were worth their weight in gold.

"Who?"

"Fritz Geissler."

Angelica frowned and shook her head. "I don't know him. Why?"

Damn, she looked like she was telling the truth. Her eyes were unveiled and met my gaze without faltering. "Your husband never mentioned him?"

"No. Never. Who is he?"

Could she seriously not know her husband's real name? I shrugged. "I just thought it might be a name from your husband's past."

"He doesn't speak of his past. He has very painful memories before coming to California."

Oh, that was telling. "What sort of memories?"

"His father abused him. Will doesn't like me to bring it up. Anything about his life in Michigan. He says his life began here in California."

Interesting cover story. So far as I knew, Fritz Geissler had had a very happy childhood and home life, in both Chicago and Lake Geneva. "When did he come here?" I asked.

"Nineteen ninety-seven. He was twenty-five."

I bit my lips together. Seventeen years ago. Fritz also would have been twenty-five seventeen years ago. The two disparate stories lined up. "What month?"

Angelica fluttered her hand in the air. "I don't know. July? August?"

Fritz Geissler had fled Lake Geneva in July, 1997.

I opened my portfolio and withdrew a color photocopy of William Read's driver's license. I didn't know how he'd established his false identification. Perhaps I'd never know. Geissler's transition into William Read was flawless. But I knew with every fiber of my being that the two men were one and the same.

I handed the photocopy to Angelica. "Is this your husband's driver's license?"

Her dark eyes brushed over the page. "Yes. This is my husband. William Read."

I sighed. This was the part where I had to break her delicately preserved bubble of hope. It sucked and I hated it. "I made this photocopy from the ID found in the wallet of the victim. The man who was found in Geneva Lake."

Angelica stared at the sheet of paper for several seconds. Then her eyes flashed to me. They were full of daggers. "You lie," she said. Her voice shook, tears threatening. "I don't know why you lie, but you lie." She threw the paper on the floor and buried her face in her hands as she cried. "He's in Las Vegas! He's at a conference. He's coming home tomorrow."

I sat with my arms folded across my lap and toyed with the badge clipped to my belt. Pulled it out. Let it snap back. Softly, so I didn't interrupt Angelica's cry. I never knew what to do when people were crying. I wasn't that cop who let strangers weep on my shoulder. Especially when they might be accessories to a crime. Like multi-million-dollar burglaries. She could just be a damn good actress, after all. Did she seriously know nothing about her husband's real past? Or was she just lying beautifully?

"I'm very sorry, Mrs. Read," I said when the woman's tears let up.

"I don't understand," she said. "He was in Las Vegas. Why would he be in Wisconsin?"

"You said your husband never spoke of his past. But did he ever mention a Bobby Markham? Or Jason Thomlin?"

"No. I have never heard of them."

I withdrew a photo from my portfolio. One of Jason. He was holding up a prize walleye—had to have been a good fifteen pounds and thirty-two, thirty-three inches. A great catch. "Have you ever seen this man? That photo is seventeen years old, but did your husband know anyone who looks even a little like him?"

Angelica shook her head. "I've never seen him."

I was actually beginning to believe her. How had Geissler managed to keep a secret like this from her for so many years? The man was a master. I pulled another photograph out of my file—Fritz standing with Jason and Bobby on the Markham pier. Taken two or three years before Bobby was killed and Fritz and Jason ran. I handed it to Angelica without saying a word. Just watched her reaction.

Angelica stared down at the photo. Her brows wavered.

"You've never seen this photograph of your husband before?"

She shook her head.

"But that *is* your husband?"

The woman raised her dark eyes. "Why do you have a picture of my husband?"

"That photo was taken in Lake Geneva, Wisconsin, in 1995. The other men in the photo were his best friends—Bobby Markham and Jason Thomlin."

"In Lake Geneva ...?"

"Bobby Markham—the man with the dark hair—was a burglar. Specialized in bank break-ins. He died in a shootout with police in Lake Geneva after one of his jobs went sour."

Angelica's hand shook. "If you think my husband had anything to do with this—"

"I'm sorry, Mrs. Read. I know he did. He and Jason Thomlin fled. There's been a warrant for them this whole time. But they vanished into thin air. Until now."

Angelica shook her head, tears gathering again. "You are wrong. My husband is a good man and a good father. He would never break the law."

I leaned forward in my chair. "All I want is to know where Jason Thomlin is. He's the last living member of the ring. He may have killed your husband."

Angelica slapped the photo down on the table. "I do not know your Jason Thompson—or whoever he is." She picked up the photocopied ID and slapped that down, too. "I do not know about millions of dollars." She shoved the papers across the glass toward me. "I've never heard of Lake Geneva. And I do not know who your murdered man is. But he is *not* my husband. Will is in *Las Vegas*. And he is coming home *tomorrow*." She stood up and pointed to the door. "You may go now."

I stood, too, but made no move to exit. "Mrs. Read, I know this hurts terribly. Clearly you didn't know anything about your husband's past, and I'm sorry I had to break it to you at this delicate time. But if you want to see justice done to your husband's murderer, you'd do best to cooperate with us. Please, where is Jason Thomlin?"

Angelica skewered me with a piercing stare. "Look me in the eyes," she said, a hand on her hip and her expression deadly earnest.

I did.

"My husband's name is William Read. He is in Las Vegas at the Quinton Hotel. And I have never, ever heard of Fritz or Bobby or your Jason what's-his-name. You have the wrong man. Now leave me alone."

I eyed the woman for a moment, wanting to throw a few judo moves at her to wake her up. Instead, I quietly stowed my papers in my portfolio. "If Jason Thomlin *does* contact you, call the police. He may not have your best interests in mind." I left my card on the table. "Then call me."

"Go," Angelica repeated, her face unchanged.

I went.

Back in my rental, I dropped my portfolio onto the car seat beside me. What had I learned? Nothing. Nothing that would tell me where to so much as begin looking for Jason. Angelica Read was truly ignorant. Of everything. Including her husband's death. Hell, she'd figure that out eventually.

"Women are bitches," I muttered as I cranked the key in the ignition.

## CHAPTER TWENTY-SEVEN
## RYAN

I didn't like Bailey's house any better the second time. At closer inspection, the stairs to the cement porch were chipped and the paint on the door was peeling. I rang the cracked plastic doorbell and wondered how this home had been approved for foster care. But I reminded myself that social services was always desperate for foster homes—and not to judge people based on the quality of their doorbells. My own apartment didn't look much better.

The door opened a crack. Bailey stood looking up at me. Wow. That really was a shiner.

"Hi, Bailey. You busy?" I asked.

"Um ... I guess not. Why?"

"Just thought I'd check in on you. Can I come in?"

Bailey stared at me blankly. She finally opened the door all the way, turned her back on me, and walked inside. I took it she meant for me to follow.

The smell of cigarette smoke hung in the air. Months' worth of outdated magazines littered the coffee table. The walls were stark white, the furniture left over from the eighties. The only wall art in the entire room was a page torn from a calendar sporting a red Corvette, a skimpily-clad blond, and the word *July*. It was pinned to the wall above the TV. It disgusted me to see it—which struck me as odd. Ordinarily, the sight of female flesh would have interested me. But not in the house of a man who claimed to be a father. Especially the foster father of a teenage girl. I suddenly liked Bud Weber even less than I had before.

Bailey curled up in a recliner that dwarfed her and focused her attention on the TV, which was playing some sort of wildlife documentary. I eyed the pink-and-orange floral sofa and bravely perched on the very edge. No telling how many years of broken potato chips were smashed into that upholstery. Ignoring the TV, I started talking.

"I checked for you at the Mailboat," I said, "but they told me it was your day off."

She nodded. Her eyes were on the documentary. I had the distinct feeling I wasn't even there.

"They also said I might find you at the Geneva Bar and Grill."

"Not today," she said.

"You work there part-time?"

She nodded.

"As a waitress?"

She nodded.

"Do you enjoy it?"

A shrug.

I was getting nowhere fast. I tapped my foot and changed the direction of the conversation. "How have you been, Bailey?" I asked.

"Good."

*Good,* she said. Meanwhile, she was staring out at the world through a blaring black eye. "Having a good summer so far?" I asked.

Bailey smiled and nodded and looked at me briefly. It was the first time I had seen her smile. She should do it more often. It really lit up her face. But glancing around this place she called home ... I didn't blame her for keeping her smile in storage. There was no warmth here. No heart.

"So tell me," I said, "are you doing all right after what happened the other day?"

Her eyes flashed to me as if I'd caught her doing something red-handed.

"I mean, finding a dead body is pretty disturbing," I elaborated. "Are you handling it all right?"

Bailey looked relieved. She shrugged. "I'm okay."

I wondered what she thought I'd meant. What happened the other day that she didn't want me to know the truth about? Her black eye? I would get to that part. But not yet. I needed to build up that rapport Wade thought she and I had.

"You have a counselor, right? Through the foster care system?" I asked.

She nodded.

"Do you need to see him or her? I can get you an appointment."

Bailey chewed the inside of her cheek before shaking her head. "I'm okay."

"Really?"

She nodded. "Really."

Apparently nothing ever phased her. Not even discovering a dead body. Did she even have a soul left?

"Well, if you change your mind, you can call me any time. My offer still stands. I'll make the appointment for you."

"Okay."

I motioned towards her face. "Looks like you had a little accident there."

"I hit the Mailboat when I fell in." She said it quickly. It sounded rehearsed. This was clearly what she didn't want me to know about.

I nodded. "I've read your accident report, as a matter of fact. While I was down at the Mailboat pier. Are you sure that's how it happened?"

Bailey nodded.

"Are you having problems with anyone?"

She shook her head. "It was just an accident."

"Who do you like to hang out with?"

"The kids at the cruise line," she said.

"Like who?" I asked.

She shifted her shoulder. "Just everyone. We work together."

"That's not the same as hanging out," I noted. "Don't you have any friends?"

Another shrug. "I don't need any."

The more I knew about Bailey, the bleaker the portrait that was painted. "You seriously don't have anyone you consider a friend?"

She chewed her lip. "Nah. Not really."

"Why not?" I asked.

She finally made eye contact with me. With a sting in her voice, she said, "I'm just going to move anyway. Why hang out with anybody?"

"You know you're moving? You've got a new placement?"

"No." The way she said it, the word *moron* was implied. "I always move. This is my twelfth placement."

I winced. Twelve placements ... in eleven years. No wonder she didn't make friends. She was right—there was no guarantee of keeping them. It was pointless.

"So, I don't suppose you have a boyfriend?"

She raised an eyebrow, as much as to say, *Are you kidding?*

I quickly moved on. "Anybody you don't like?"

"I like everyone fine."

*Good, okay, fine.* She didn't love anyone. She didn't hate anyone. She was just *good, okay, fine.*

"How about your foster dad? Are you happy in this placement?"

To my surprise, Bailey's face lit up with a winning smile. "Oh, yes."

Her response struck me speechless for a moment. At last, something she loved ... and it was the lazy bum who let his yard go to weeds?

"Tell me more about him. What's his name?"

"Bud Weber."

"Do you have a foster mother, too?"

She shook her head. "I don't think he's ever been married."

"Is he seeing anyone?"

"No."

That struck me as odd. Why did a bachelor want to foster a teenage girl? It was perfectly legal for a single man to foster children of any age and either sex. And social services performed thorough background checks on every applicant. But my gut was screaming that there was something wrong about this placement.

"Does he treat you well?"

"Yep."

"Has he ever hit you?"

"No."

Right there. She lied. Almost everything else she'd said up to this point had been the truth. But right then when she said "no," she lied. Her eyes wavered for a split second. Her shoulders caved in a fraction of an inch. She gave herself away. Bud Weber *was* abusing her.

I glanced at the TV, wishing it weren't there to create distractions in our conversation. I leaned closer. "Bailey, does he do anything else to you? Does he touch you?"

She pulled a face and shook her head. But her cheeks turned the faintest shade of pink.

"Does he make you have sex?"

"He wouldn't do that." Her mouth moved, but the rest of her body was immobile, her eyes fixed on the television screen.

"Did he tell you he'd hurt you again if you said anything?"

She made a disgusted expression and looked at me. "No, because he doesn't hit me and he doesn't make me have sex. He's a great guy. I seriously want to stay with him."

"And yet you're convinced you're going to move?"

She turned her eyes back to the documentary. "I always move."

I glanced around the soul-less house. The blank walls. The second-hand furniture. The worn carpet. "You really like it here?"

She nodded definitively. "Yep."

I wasn't so sure she was lying anymore. Something about this latest declaration felt besmattered with truth. Though it was beyond me what she'd love about a place like this and the man who lived here.

I reached into my shirt pocket and pulled out my business card. "Bailey, I want you to let me know if you ever feel uncomfortable here, okay? That's my cell number. Call me any time. Day or night. It makes no difference to me."

She took the card and shrugged. "Sure."

"Okay." I stood up. "Thanks, Bailey. I'm just checking on you. I want to make sure you're happy and in the best home."

"I am," she said with another winning smile.

I still couldn't figure that.

Bailey didn't follow me to the door. I let myself out.

Something wasn't right about what had just happened. Her foster father was clearly abusing her, and she was clearly protecting him—for reasons of her own.

My investigation wasn't done yet.

## CHAPTER TWENTY-EIGHT
## RYAN

I walked into the Geneva Bar and Grill, feeling like a cop in the middle of a bar—which is exactly what I was. At this time of the afternoon, only a handful of patrons filled a scattering of tables. Country music played over the sound system, and no less than three TVs showed a baseball game in full swing. The Cubs were ahead, three-to-two.

A forty-something woman trying to look like a twenty-something breezed by in a mini skirt, lots of makeup, and a blouse that could have had at least two more buttons done up. After viewing Bud Weber's wall art at his house, I was equally unimpressed with his employee. Bailey worked here part-time—and I hoped she never viewed this particular woman as a role model.

I shook my head in wonder. What was happening to me? The old Ryan would have been delighted by this female specimen.

"Have a seat, hon. Be right with ya," the woman said.

I stepped forward to halt her progress. "Is Bud in?" I decided using his full name would make it sound too official.

She stopped and eyed my uniform. "Yeah. He's in the bar." She jerked her head.

"Thanks."

I made for a neon sign over a doorway and climbed three steps. The lights were darker, the music louder, and the TVs bigger. A knot of men sat at the bar on stools, beer bottles parked in front of them at various stages of completion.

One man stood behind the bar, in the middle of telling some story, while the other guys hung on every word. The bartender was at least six two and could have played tackle in his younger years. Any imposing body mass he may have once possessed was now concentrated primarily in a beer belly, which strained at his black tee shirt. I couldn't follow the story the man was trying to tell—half of it was just profanity—but his audience snickered in anticipation, and when the punchline finally hit, they exploded with laughter.

One of them looked up and noticed me. "Aw, crap, don't tell me it's illegal now to drink beer in the afternoon."

The bartender cuffed the back of his head. "Shut up, Tony." He moved away from the beer drinkers. "Hey, officer, what can I do for ya? Can I get you anything?" He spoke with a thick Chicago accent.

I smiled. "No thanks. I'm just here to ask you a few questions."

"My liquor license is all straight, officer. My business license, too."

"It's not that."

"Oh. Well, sit down." He motioned to the bar stools. "Crap, you can have a soda, can't you? What do you want?"

I stayed standing. "I'm fine. Thank you, though."

Bud hesitated, as if weighing whether he were in trouble. He finally offered his hand over the bar. "I don't think we've met. I'm Bud Weber. I own this place."

I took his hand. "Officer Ryan Brandt."

"Good to meet you. You don't mind if I have a drink, do you?"

"No, not at all."

He pulled down a glass from a shelf behind the bar and filled it at the tap. Then he leaned on his forearms with the glass between his thick palms. "So, what can I do for you?"

"I thought we'd talk about Bailey."

A smile lit up Bud's face. "Oh, she's a sweet kid. Foster care's the smartest thing I've ever done. Never had much of a home life before I got Bailey." He took a long haul from his glass.

That was not the kind of response I'd anticipated. I thought for sure I'd get a guilty look. Some signal, however slight, that he'd rather not talk about his relationship with Bailey.

"Does she give you any trouble?" I asked.

Bud wagged his head. "Naw. She's like a little mouse. Ya hardly know she's there half the time. Not like these foster kids you hear about, painting graffiti and shoplifting and crap. She don't have a bad bone in her body."

I smiled in agreement. "She's a good kid." I went in for the kill. "What can you tell me about this black eye she's got?"

Bud frowned. "What black eye?"

I hadn't expected him to flat-out deny it. "The black eye I saw she had just fifteen minutes ago."

Bud looked taken aback. "What the hell? When did she get a black eye?"

That's what I wanted *him* to answer. I evaded his question. "It's hard to miss. I'm surprised you didn't notice it."

"She didn't have no black eye last time I saw her."

"When was that?" I asked.

He looked abashed. "Two nights ago. I know that ain't ideal, but our schedules just haven't been lining up. I work late; she works early." Bud shifted his forearms on the counter. "But how do *you* know about it? What, did she call you?" Bud straightened up. "What the hell did she tell you? Did she say *I* had somethin' to do with it?"

"She didn't call us," I said. "One of her coworkers was concerned and wanted us to look into it."

Bud looked hot around the collar. "Well, you can tell whoever-it-is that he ain't got no business stirring up trouble where there isn't any. Look, I know I'm a little rough around the edges. Maybe I ain't exactly your stereotypical foster parent. And I told them social workers up front, I didn't want no stream of kids running through my house, three and four at a time. I just wanted the one, and they gave me Bailey, and it's worked out real good. Ask her yourself."

"I did," I said.

"Well then, she told you. She's real happy."

So she said. I still wasn't convinced "happy" was the right word.

"What got you interested in foster care, Mr. Weber?"

He shrugged. "I was lonely, I guess. I know what you're gonna say—why didn't I get married or somethin'? Well, damn, no woman wants a big lug like me. But kids? They just look up to you like you're the world, you know? And I just wanted to do something that'd make a difference in somebody's life. That's why."

I nodded as if I agreed with every word that had just slipped out of his lips. "Damn good reasons," I said. "Look, I've never been a father, but I understand raising a teenager can be challenging."

"Sure," he agreed.

"Sometimes you have to set them straight. I get it. That's called parenting. Now, I'm not here to tell you how to do it," I said with a hand on my bullet-proof vest. "It's hard enough, especially when it's not your own child. Sometimes they think that means they don't have to listen to you. You have to keep after them. Maybe even be a little hard on them. For their own good, right?"

He straightened up, palms sliding across the counter top. "Oh, not with Bailey. I tell you, that Bailey is just a little angel. I've never had to so much as raise my voice with her."

Dang it. I was hoping to lead him into a confession. "You mean to tell me you've never had to punish her?"

"Nope. Not once. Can't understand why no one adopts her. She's just perfect in every way."

Except she didn't have the least spark of life left in her.

"Why don't you adopt her yourself?" I asked.

"As a matter of fact, I've been thinkin' about it," he said.

*Over my dead body,* I thought. I knew in my gut that he was abusing Bailey, and I'd adopt the girl myself before letting her go to him to be misused for the rest of her life.

"I don't know how she came by that black eye," the man went on, "but if anybody hit her, I'd be the first to pound his ass into the ground. She's like my own, you know? And I don't mind sayin', I resent anybody suggesting I would ever raise a finger against her—whoever this dodo is at the cruise line who's raisin' cain. I don't want nobody taking that kid away from me. She's like family now, you know what I mean?"

"Sure, Mr. Weber," I said. "I just needed to know if you knew anything about how she came by that bruise."

"Well, didn't you ask her?"

"She says it happened when she fell off the Mailboat."

Bud slapped the counter. "Well, there you go. This whole investigation of yours is just a big waste of time. She told you herself. Who the hell's tryin' to make a big deal out of this?"

"No one," I assured him. "Just checking, you know. We all care about Bailey."

Weber rubbed a meaty hand across the back of his neck. "Right. I know. Look, I'm sorry if I lost it a little. It's just I don't want no one taking her away from me."

"I understand." More than he knew. Abusers were, at their root, consumed with the need to control.

Bud blew a sigh, puffing his cheeks. "Well ... are ya sure I can't get you a drink?"

"No, thanks. I'll be on my way. Thanks for giving me a minute, Mr. Weber."

"Yeah. You know, you can check on her any time."

"Thanks." I tipped my head with a meaningful glance and added, "I will."

I walked out to my patrol car. I was still itching to pull out my handcuffs, but with both Bailey and Bud denying foul play, my hands were tied. I had nothing that would stick in court. Just hunches and gut reactions.

But something just wasn't right.

## CHAPTER TWENTY-NINE
## BAILEY

When I got sick of watching TV and reading all day, I headed to my room and shut the door. Humphrey would want to get out again and sniff the yarn on my quilt. And Bud wouldn't be home yet until late, like usual.

I plopped onto my bed and set my book on the corner of the end table. I didn't really like days off. Days off from the restaurant were peachy, but days off from the cruise line were the worst. I would have happily worked seven days a week, from the early-morning Mailboat shift to the late-night sunset cruise. I loved being around the boats. Sometimes I thought they were the only thing that made me happy. I closed my eyes and smiled as I pictured the queenly stern-wheeled paddle boats, white in the sunshine, and the slender, gleaming yachts that were built at the turn of the last century, and the little wooden cabin cruiser.

And the Mailboat. I loved the Mailboat in particular. It was a hulking sort of boat—not pretty, exactly, thanks to its boxy lines. But it was beautiful to me, stately in a coat of navy blue and white paint and warm wood trim. There was nothing like the Mailboat cruise. The thrill of the jump. The ballet of boat and pier; wind, wave, and hull; captain and jumper.

Captain and jumper.

I laid back on my denim quilt and flopped my arms out wide. What was it like to have a dad? Or a grandfather? Or just family? You know, the kind that actually stuck around your whole life. The kind of family who were there every year when you passed another grade in school—instead of flaking off to God-knows-where and dumping you off on another family. What was it like to have the kind of family who were proud of you and everything you ever accomplished, even if it was just wrapping toilet paper around a mouse's leg and keeping it alive in an end table drawer? Not to mention getting A's in every class and winning a much-sought-after job as a mail jumper.

Bud didn't care how I did in school, and only let me take the cruise line job reluctantly, with the stipulation that I also leave enough time in my schedule to work one or two nights a week at the restaurant.

I leaned on my elbow and opened the Executive Recovery Suite. Humphrey was curled up in a little ball in his toilet paper roll. He woke up and twitched his whiskers as his tube-shaped bed rocked back and forth. Then he stretched, squeaked, and slid out, looking up at me with big, black eyes. I scooped him up carefully and set him on top of my pillow.

The bandage looked really good—surprisingly. He ran little circles between the yarn tufts without favoring his leg at all. He was getting better. I couldn't wait to tell Tommy.

He would be so proud of me.

My door burst open so loudly I nearly choked. I scooped Humphrey up, basically tossed him back into the drawer, and slammed it shut. I whirled in time to see Bud storm into my room. He grabbed my arm and stuck his face in mine.

"Who did you tell?"

My mind scrambled. This wasn't about Humphrey. Something else. Some fact I'd let slip to someone. What fact? Who had I told, and what had I said? Try as I might, I couldn't think of a thing.

"Tell what?" I asked in a shaking voice.

*Smack.* His palm came across my cheek. "Don't be smart with me, kid."

Tears ran down my face as the sting set in. Not the physical one. I mean, sure, it hurt. But it was even more excruciating on the inside. Something about being slapped. It made me feel ... like dirt. Like less than dirt. Like how Humphrey probably felt having giant cans of peas and corn shoved at him. Like my existence simply did not matter. Like I should just curl up in a puff of smoke and vanish forever and quit making other people's lives so miserable.

It hurt worse knowing that Bud wasn't drunk this time. I couldn't blame it on the alcohol. He was totally sober, and he hated me. Like a book you just wanted to rip in two down the spine and fling across the room.

"I'm sorry," I said. "What did I do wrong?" Apologize first. Figure it out later. Apologize. Apologize. Apologize ... Calm the beast ... Anything to make him stop hating me.

"You complained to somebody," he said, his voice as big as a thunderstorm. "Somebody at the cruise line. Told them I gave you a black eye. Did I ever give you a black eye?"

"No. I hit my face on the Mailboat." At that moment, I believed my own lie. I believed with every fiber of my being that I'd hit my face on the handrail. Anything to keep Bud from hitting me again. Anything to earn his favor back.

"That wasn't all you told them, was it? You told them about our little secret, didn't you?"

The sex. He called it "our little secret," as if it were something special.

"I didn't tell anything!"

"Who did you tell?"

"No one."

He twisted my arm until a piercing yelp came out of my mouth.

116

"You sure?"

"Yes! Ow! Please, let me go!"

He twisted harder. I went down to my knees.

*"Tommy!"* I yelled.

"That boat captain?"

"Yes!"

"You told him?"

"No. He saw my black eye. He asked about it. I told him I hit my face on the boat when I missed my jump. Please, let me go!"

He shoved me so I fell back on my rear, my back against the bed. I rubbed my arm and sniffled.

Bud's eyes slowly wandered to my desk. He nodded. "What's in the drawer?"

My blood ran cold. "Nothing."

"Nothing, huh?" He walked up to my desk and slowly pulled open the drawer. I heard a peep and pictured twitching whiskers and a toilet paper roll rocking back and forth.

Bud eyed me menacingly. "You call this 'nothing'? You keep a filthy little rodent in my house and you call it 'nothing'?"

I didn't answer. Just sat on the floor gaping.

Bud picked up my book from the corner of the end table. Lowered it slowly into the drawer. I heard a squeak followed by a sickening crunch. Then silence.

Bud turned back to me. Slid his belt out of the loops. "Now," he said. "What other lies have you been tellin'?"

## CHAPTER THIRTY
## MONICA

"Back already?" Lehman leaned back in his office chair, stretching his back and displaying both his paunch and his detective badge clipped to his belt. "How was L.A.?"

"Shove it up your ass," I said, slapping my portfolio down on my desk.

"Not good, huh?"

I dropped into my own chair and booted up my computer. "She's psycho," I replied, meaning Geissler's wife—or Read's wife, or whoever she was. I didn't think she even knew who she was. I snarked at my own joke, leaving Lehman completely in the dark and enjoying it.

I logged into my email. The only thing that could have redeemed my time in California would have been a trip to the beach, but the department wasn't paying for that. It was going to be bad enough, trying to explain to the chief how I'd spent hundreds of department dollars, with very little to show in return. If Angelica Read had any information on the Bobby Markham gang, or any idea where to find Jason Thomlin, she wasn't saying.

I sipped from my coffee mug and browsed down the email subject lines, mentally prioritizing them. My eyes widened when I spied one from the phone company I'd called yesterday. I opened it immediately. That was about the fastest I'd ever seen a phone company reply to a court order for a customer's cell phone data. Normally, I didn't even bother with the cell phone companies. Normally, I could power up a phone and see what was on it. But Fritz Geissler's phone had spent eight hours at the bottom of the lake and was as dead as he was—way past the rice treatment method.

An attached PDF listed every call he'd made in the past two weeks, and his location at the time of his call. Most of them were placed and received in Los Angeles. But a string at the very end showed him at Denver, then Chicago, then Lake Geneva. The number he'd called in each instance was Angelica Read's.

I sighed and shook my head. There was ample proof that her husband was the dead man. She was simply out of her mind with grief.

One phone call, sent to his phone the day he died, originated in Washington, D.C. It looked like the major outlier. I made a note of the phone number.

The text messages in a separate PDF were all uninteresting—other than a conversation with his wife saying the conference was going well and he hadn't had time yet to play the slot machines.

He'd sent that from Lake Geneva.

I lifted my eyebrows. Well, that was telling. Fritz Geissler had lied to his wife. She really did believe he was at a conference in Las Vegas. That meant it was likely she truly didn't know a thing about his past in Lake Geneva. His history with the Bobby Markham gang. I couldn't imagine how he'd done it, but he'd lived a lie with her for the duration of their marriage. He had left Fritz Geissler behind in Lake Geneva the night Bobby died, and been born again as William Read.

No wonder she didn't know who Jason Thomlin was.

I couldn't help but think that if Geissler hadn't died of strangulation, he would have died of stress. No one could live a double life without rotting from the inside out.

Which naturally led me to the question: What had brought Geissler back to Lake Geneva in the first place?

I turned my attention to a handful of audio files—the contents of his voicemail. I opened the first one and hit play. It was a note from one of his business colleagues. The next was a client. The third was from his wife, reminding him to pick up the kids after school. On and on they went. None of them seemed to have anything to do with the case. They were all boring as hell.

Just as I was thinking about another cup of coffee, I opened the last file. The status bar filled with color as the audio played over my speakers.

*"Fritz, it's Jason. Don't go to the cops, do you hear me? Do not go to the cops. I'll be there in a matter of hours. Don't do anything you'll regret later."*

I sat straighter. Jason. I was listening to Jason. I dragged the marker back to the beginning, turned up the volume on my speakers, and played the file again. My heart beat with anticipation. I had evidence that Jason had contacted Fritz. I had evidence that Fritz had been planning to turn himself in. Better yet, I had Jason's phone number. The call from D.C. aligned with the date and time of the voicemail.

Jason Thomlin had been hiding in Washington, D.C. And he'd been in Lake Geneva.

I made extra copies of both the PDFs and the audio files, and got up to talk to Wade.

Jason could have killed Fritz to prevent him from revealing their secrets. And if his work wasn't done, he could still be in Lake Geneva.

## CHAPTER THIRTY-ONE
## BAILEY

I wish I could say I was a big girl and I didn't cry about
Humphrey. But I did. I cried about him. And I prayed with
all my heart that Tommy wouldn't ask how progress was
going in the Executive Recovery Suit. It wasn't a suit
anymore. It was just an end table drawer. And it made me
sick to think about the whole thing.

Ordinarily, I have no qualms about the weather guy
predicting sunny and eighty-five. Today I did. My long-
sleeved tee shirt was already miserable. But I didn't have a
choice. My heart sank with jealousy when I walked up the
pier to the Mailboat and saw Tommy dressed in shorts and
short sleeves.

He unlocked the Mailboat, then turned and eyed me up
and down. "Hope you brought something cooler. It's gonna
be warm today."

I shrugged. "I'll be fine."

"What, are you chilly?"

I nodded.

"Catch cold after falling in the other day?"

I nodded again. Nice of him to provide lies for me so I
wouldn't have to make them up myself.

Tommy laughed. "When you fall in, you fall in. How's
that black eye of yours doing?"

I shrugged. "Still pretty." I knew he still didn't believe I'd hit my face on the Mailboat while missing my jump.

"Well, I can see that. Is it still painful?"

I shook my head. "Nah. It's good." By comparison. Other parts of my body hurt worse.

Tommy picked up the stack of newspapers sitting at his feet on the pier and led the way into the Mailboat. I dropped off my backpack on a chair up front then headed toward the two skinny little cupboards near the bathrooms. As I poked around for a roll of paper towel and the window cleaner, Tommy came up behind me.

"Would you hand me the broom, Bailey?"

I reached for the long, black handle. Tommy held his hand out to accept it—then grabbed my sleeve and pulled it up to my elbow. The two red welts on my arm, already turning yellow and purple and blue, stared out at the world, blinking in bewilderment like a couple of yellow and purple and blue things.

Tommy gave me a cold, hard stare that made me wish I could fit inside the six-inch wide cupboard. It was bad enough being belted by Bud last night. Making Tommy upset was, like, a kajillion times worse.

"Come here." Tommy jerked his head toward the stacks of plastic chairs. He grabbed a couple from the pile and set them in the middle of the floor.

I stood where I was like a zombie. A zombie with a bottle of cleaner in one hand. I managed to eek out one word. "Windows?"

"It's not even seven o'clock yet. Sit down."

I slid into the chair opposite Tommy, clinging to the window cleaner as if it might bring me good luck.

Tommy leaned his elbows on his knees and stared at me hard. I looked to see if he had anything like a belt in his hands. I don't know why I needed to check for that. I couldn't ever picture him actually decking somebody. But I just ... I had to check. The fact that he was angry at me

122

made me want to throw myself into the lake. And get tangled in a rope all over again. And drown this time.

"This is the second time you've lied to me," he said.

His hands weren't balling into fists or anything. Okay, so maybe he wasn't going to hit me. But he sure as heck was going to report me to Robb and get me fired. I told myself to be a big girl and not cry.

Yeah right.

"I want a straight answer from you this time. Who hit you?"

My mind raced. What kind of story could I make up that he might actually believe? Between panic and a bad imagination, all I managed to do was stare at him blankly.

"Was it your foster dad?"

My throat tightened like a Venus flytrap snapping shut. How did he know? Not just about Bud decking me—but that I was in foster care at all?

A tiny little voice wanted to say, *Yes it was my foster dad,* but my big girl voice told it to shut up. *You know what'll happen if anyone finds out. You already blew it by letting Tommy see your bruises. DON'T let this go any further. Failure ISN'T an option.*

I found myself shaking my head.

"Then who did it?"

Again, like the brilliant orator I was, I sat and stared.

Tommy frowned and shook his head. "Why are you trying to protect this person? If someone's hurting you, you need to stand up for yourself. You need to say something. Your social worker can help you."

I tried not to flinch, but I did. I flinched. The words "social worker" instantly conjured a number of faces I'd known over the years. They were all pretty nice, for the most part.

But I lived in a sort of fear vortex, the operative words being "social worker." They could drop down on you at any moment, smile sweetly, and tell you to pack your stuff. "It's moving day," one of them told me once, and I've hated the phrase ever since. "Moving day" usually happens every two or three years. Maybe every six months. Maybe after a couple of weeks. Sometimes the move is for the better. Sometimes for the worse. It's a coin toss. Once, it meant moving back in with my mom. She held me tight and promised they'd never take me away again.

They came for me two months later. It was the last time I ever saw her.

"Bailey? Aren't you going to say anything?"

I wanted to say a zillion things, and they all wanted to be said at once. I didn't know where to start. Or if I should start at all. I wanted him to understand. To understand why I didn't want "help."

Because "help" would mean "moving day" again. And "moving day" could literally mean to anyplace in the county. It could mean, like, not Lake Geneva anymore.

It could mean no Mailboat anymore.

It could mean no Tommy anymore.

I didn't care if Bud blacked both eyes, both arms, both legs, and knocked out all my teeth—if it meant I could keep Tommy. He was the first person in my life who felt ... permanent. I mean, gees, he'd been showing up at this boat at seven in the morning, every morning, every summer for, like, fifty years. If that wasn't permanent, what was?

In a flash, I finally realized why I loved Tommy so much. Why I daydreamed that he cared about me as much as I cared about him. Why I even wished he were my family.

Just because he was always there. And always would be. Just like the Mailboat itself.

But for some reason, I couldn't say any of that out loud. He would hate me if he knew how much I cared about him. Decent young ladies don't go around throwing themselves at the first nice person they meet. Even if they've been waiting to meet that person their whole life.

When I still failed to provide an answer, Tommy sighed, sat up, and rubbed his palms across his shorts. He changed the subject slightly. "What happened to your parents?"

Oh, God, I hated this question. Usually asked by nosy kids at school who would proceed to torment you about it till the day you died. But in the grand scheme of things, it was actually less painful right now to talk about my parents than to entertain the possibility of "moving day."

"My mom's dead."

"And your dad?"

I shrugged.

"Oh." Tommy looked down.

Yeah. 'Nuff said on that topic.

"How long have you been in foster care?" he asked.

"Since I was five."

"Five?" He looked at me incredulously. "Why aren't you adopted?"

'Cuz I'm pathetic, I wanted to say. "I wasn't available until after my mom died. When I was twelve. No one wants to adopt a twelve-year-old." I passed the bottle of window cleaner back and forth between my hands. Like it didn't matter.

"Oh." Tommy frowned. "So ...?"

"My mom was in prison. She OD'd on drugs the last time they let her out."

"Ah." He rubbed his palms on his shorts again. "I'm sorry, Bailey."

I shrugged and kept playing ping-pong with the spray bottle. But actually, it was the first time anyone had offered condolences on the sheer patheticness of my life. It was kind of awesome, as if I hadn't deserved all this crap. And that was just so weird, I didn't know how to respond.

"Her name was Kalli." I don't know why I said it. The words just kinda slipped out. But now that I'd started, I kept going. "With a K. I always thought it was a really pretty name. I kinda wish she'd named me 'Kalli,' too." I stopped and glanced up at Tommy. "I guess that's dumb, though, isn't it?" Yeah, it was dumb. When would I ever remember that opening my mouth was a universally bad idea?

Tommy shrugged. "It used to be done a lot. Naming a daughter after her mother."

I tilted my head. "For real?"

"Oh, a long time ago, back in the olden days. You still see it now and again."

Tommy would know. He knew tons about "the olden days"—including, like, every last thing there was to know about Lake Geneva, probably right down to everybody's name. I liked that he didn't think it was dumb that I wanted to be named after my mother.

"Bailey's a pretty name, too," he said. "And she gave it to you."

I'd really never thought of that before. But now it dawned on me ... it was the only thing I had from her. I'd lost a lot of crap between all those moving days. I didn't have a single thing left from my childhood.

Except my name. The name my mother gave to me. And Tommy thought it was pretty.

Something inside me glowed. Something that hadn't ever glowed before.

Tommy stirred, like he was about to get up. "If you, ah ... If you change your mind about how you got those bruises, you can ... you can talk to your social worker. Okay?" He stood up and walked away, leaving a plastic chair staring at me blankly.

Um, that was kinda weird. But by now, I was pretty much used to people peeling off at random. I didn't dwell on it. But talking to my social worker?

Yeah. No. That wasn't going to happen.

## CHAPTER THIRTY-TWO
## MONICA

I rang Markham's doorbell for the fifth time before giving up and huffing back down the white steps toward my unmarked SUV. I knew the doorbell wasn't broken. I could hear it resonating throughout the entire house like a bell in a Gothic steeple. Where was that millionaire? His life was on the line, and he was off boating on the lake or something.

Come to think of it, perhaps that was exactly where he was.

I aborted the mission for my SUV and made a new course for the back of the mansion.

*Front.* Damn. Even I'd forgotten.

As I crossed the ocean of perfectly manicured grass, I spotted two figures reclining on deck furniture on the pier. Markham's two boats—the steam launch and the classic wooden speed boat—bobbed placidly on either side of them. Markham leaned out of his Adirondack chair to fill a glass from a pitcher full of brown liquid, ice, and lemon slices.

I sighed and shook my head at the sight of him and his next-door neighbor. Sometimes simple technology like doorbells will let you down. I let myself through the gate that separated the Lake Shore Path from the pier.

At the sound of my footfalls on the wooden boards, Markham looked over his shoulder. "Why, Detective Steele! What a pleasure to see you again." He set down the glass and the pitcher and stood.

The neighbor rose, also. Hell, what was his name? Hart. Charles, or something. There was more formality than friendliness in the man's gesture. I'd never met anyone more heavily starched or silent.

"I've been trying to call you, Mr. Markham. I keep getting your voicemail," I said.

"Oh, my deepest apologies. I like to disconnect every now and again. I left my phone up at the house." He motioned me toward a chair next to Hart. "Care for a glass of iced tea?" He reached for the pitcher.

"No, thanks. I can't stay. I've got a lot on the schedule today." We had released a forensically age-progressed photo of Jason Thomlin on the police department's Facebook page, asking our citizen force to inform us if they'd seen him. The same photo would be going out on the news at noon and again at six o'clock. I expected we'd be inundated with calls—most of them false alarms. But one or two of them might be just the tip we were looking for. They all had to be investigated.

"A policewoman's work is never done," Markham quipped.

I grinned. *Ain't that the truth.* "Anything else strange happen here since the vandalism?"

"No, no, no. It's been perfectly quiet. I really don't think there's anything to worry about."

"I hate to disagree with you. I have new evidence that gives me ample reason to believe that Jason Thomlin is in town. In light of the circumstances, I wouldn't take his threats lightly. We'll be sending extra patrols past your house. Make sure your doors are locked. In fact, it would be better if you went somewhere else until we locate him."

"Are you serious, detective?"

"Very."

"Well, I'm afraid that's quite impossible. I have to give a report to the Rotary Club tomorrow—"

"For God's sake," Hart interrupted, surprising me. "Stay with me. Jason wouldn't think of looking next door for you."

Markham appeared just as stunned as I was. He stared blankly at his neighbor for a moment before answering. "I still seriously doubt Jason is looking for me at all."

"Mr. Markham," I said, "Jason had motive for killing Fritz. He was afraid Fritz was going to go to the police with information that would have ruined them both. I know he is or was in town. I know somebody threatened you with a warning—'cleaning house.' It fits. Jason is concerned Fritz told you their secrets. He's cleaning house. Getting rid of anyone who could ruin him. I don't want to scare you, but it's my duty to notify you that you should take appropriate precautions."

Markham glanced between Hart and me, then sighed and shook his head. "I'll consider it, Detective Steele." Hart opened his mouth to object, but Markham held up his hand. "You're both forgetting something. If Jason had wanted to kill me ... he would have done it by now."

There was truth to his words. Why hadn't Jason Thomlin already made his move?

## CHAPTER THIRTY-THREE
## TOMMY

I scrubbed the sanding block back and forth, warming the birdseye maple under the friction, polishing it to a satin smoothness. Sawdust hung in the air above my workbench, illuminated by red, late-evening light streaming through paned windows. The radio by my elbow hummed the Cubs game. My thoughts seemed to hang in the air with the dust and the announcer's voice, all of them swirling together until I almost couldn't tell the one from the other.

This morning, I had been on the verge of telling Bailey to come to me if she needed anything. And at the last moment, I'd bailed out. Told her to go to her social worker. Why had I done that? I couldn't seem to grasp the answer, however hard I tried.

Noah entered my thoughts, too. Just a couple of days ago, he'd told me that Bailey was in foster care. The information had taken me completely off guard. How had I missed something so important? Something so central to Bailey's existence? What was I missing about the other kids at the cruise line? Like Noah? What did I know about him, other than that he was entering his junior year in high school?

It wouldn't have bothered me, except that this wasn't like me at all. Or it hadn't been.

Ryan Brandt strolled across my memory next, and I almost laughed. He'd been full of shenanigans when he was a boy, like stealing another kid's backpack and throwing it onto the roof of the boat. If they couldn't get it down themselves, he'd do it for them—and fall into the lake, just for a laugh. He'd been dating Monica Steele since their junior year in high school, about the same time they'd both started working for the cruise line. I knew they'd gone to prom together. I knew Ryan was on the football team and that Monica was head of the cheerleading squad and played in the marching band. I knew they'd both gone into criminal justice when they went to college. The summer after they graduated, I saw them around town on bicycle and foot patrol on their first jobs with the Lake Geneva Police Department. That same summer, they'd gotten married.

How could I know—and remember—all this about two people who had been mail jumpers of mine decades ago ... and not know that Bailey was in foster care?

When I thought about it, the answer was simple.

I used to ask.

"I figured I'd find you out here."

I looked up. Wade strolled into my garage through the open door.

I shrugged and smiled, shoving aside my thoughts. "Where else would you find me?"

"You pretty much just rotate between here and the Mailboat," Wade said.

I chuckled and threw my weight back into the swing of the sanding block.

Out of the corner of my eye, I saw Wade run his hand along the gunwale of my 1927 Chris-Craft Cadet. It sat on a trailer on one side of my two-stall garage. The Cadet was a pretty little wooden boat, the Ford Model T of classic watercraft. You could spend upwards of $40,000 to get one nowadays, but I'd bought mine in a state of disrepair. And by disrepair, I mean I wouldn't have trusted her in any body of water over six inches deep. Two years later, she was starting to look pretty good—like her old self again. The slab of birdseye maple beneath my sanding block would soon be a shiny new dashboard full of brass gauges.

"How much longer before she's seaworthy?" Wade asked.

"Well, she's seaworthy now," I replied. "She's got a hull, a helm, and a motor, and she doesn't leak. That's all you need."

Wade laughed. "Yeah, but knowing you, you'll never let her out of this garage until she's good enough to win the Miss America pageant."

I didn't deny it.

Wade found a few uncluttered inches of the workbench, brushed off the sawdust, and leaned on his elbow. Despite his care, he'd already collected a pale-colored smear on his black uniform pants. Probably from bumping against the boat. His badge and his name plate glinted in the late evening light and his gun belt squeaked as he shifted his weight. "Who's winning?" he asked, nodding at the radio.

I stared at it momentarily. It suddenly dawned on me that I didn't know. Not so much as which inning they were in. I'd been too preoccupied with my own thoughts to pay attention. "I guess I lost track," I said.

Wade laughed. "Just a sign of our old age."

I laughed with him, not wanting to confess to the tangled thoughts that had consumed my mind instead of the game.

"One of my guys checked on Bailey this afternoon."

"Oh?"

"She still says she ran into the Mailboat. Her foster dad denies even knowing she had a black eye."

I adjusted my glasses and looked up at Wade. "If you're close enough to the Mailboat to hit it with your eye, you're close enough to the Mailboat to grab the handrail. I don't buy that story for two seconds."

Wade shrugged helplessly. "Unless Bailey or Bud change their story, we don't have a case. Bailey doesn't hang out with a lot of people. We've already talked with the ones she does—just a handful of kids at the cruise line— and they know nothing. So there are no other suspects, no other witnesses, and no other sources of information."

I put down the sanding block. "Somebody hit her in the face. Whoever it was, I don't want him to ever have the chance to do it again. He's already belted her across the arms."

"What?"

"She had fresh bruises when she came to work this morning. Welts on her arms. Somebody hit her with an object of some sort."

Wade sighed heavily. "We'll look into it."

"I already asked her about it. She wouldn't tell me a word. She's scared stiff of whoever has her under his thumb."

A smile played at the corners of Wade's mouth.

I scowled at him. "Why are you smiling?"

Wade lifted his shoulder. "I don't know. It's just ... do you realize I haven't seen you this ... *alive* in years?"

"What are you talking about?" Not sure I wanted to know, I went back to the sanding block, scrubbing the dashboard with a vengeance.

Wade stirred uncomfortably. "We don't have heart-to-hearts real often," he observed. "Maybe now's as good a time as any."

"Fine. Talk your heart out."

"Are you happy, Tommy?"

What kind of a question was that? I smiled and made a sweeping gesture, encompassing my entire work bench and the Cadet behind me. "If this isn't happy, you tell me what is. Of course I'm happy. I'm seventy-five years old and still healthy enough to work. I love my job. I'm financially comfortable. I live in a great town. And I have the Mailboat."

Wade made half a smile. "Is that how you define 'happy'?"

"It's how I define 'happy' for me. My wants are simple. I don't need anything else."

"Don't you?"

"Nope. Not a thing."

"Friends?"

"Everybody knows me."

"Family?"

I shelved the sanding block in its designated place and picked up the next finer grade. "The cruise line is like family to me. You know that. I've known half the people there since they were born."

"They're great people," Wade agreed. "I don't know why you hold them all at the end of a stick."

"Who do I hold at the end of a stick?"

He shrugged, stood upright, and stuffed his hands into his pockets. "Well, I don't know. All I know is that I remember a boy named Tommy who used to be best friends with the world—not squirreled away in his garage tinkering on boats. Don't get me wrong; it's a beautiful boat. It's just that you used to make it a point of becoming friends with everybody. When we were young, you knew every new kid in school. Even took them under your wing when the other kids bullied them."

I laughed. "Nobody would dare bully you now." Shorty Wade Erickson. That's how the boys used to taunt him. Until I put him behind a bat and proved he could outrun the fastest arm on the diamond. Then he was the cool kid. Somehow the nickname stuck, even after he hit his growth spurt and outgrew us all.

"I learned how to stand on my own two feet," Wade agreed. "You taught me how. The point is, I would agree that the people at the cruise line *used* to be your family. I've never seen a man with so many sons and daughters. And then something happened. I haven't seen you take anyone under your wing for a long, long time. In fact, ... not since Jason disappeared."

I stopped sanding and sighed. I'd prefer it if Wade didn't mention Jason.

"Maybe you won't know what I'm talking about; maybe you don't even realize this. But the Tommy I used to know died when Jason skipped town. And I didn't catch a glimpse of him again until just now. The other day, when you told me you were worried about Bailey."

I stared at Wade. "You're right. I don't know what you're talking about." It was a lie. I knew exactly what he was talking about. I just didn't want to discuss it. Not now. Not when I didn't have any answers myself. Not when I felt so guilty for having no idea that one of the sweetest girls I'd ever met was being beaten by the man who was supposed to look out for her.

Wade ran a hand over his buzz-cut hair. "You changed when you lost your son."

"Wade." I locked eyes with him. "Don't talk to me about Jason."

A strained silence followed, and I realized the antagonism in my voice probably lent credence to Wade's argument. I sighed.

"Okay. Yes. I was upset with Jason. I still am. I'm upset at him for ruining his own life. Breaking his mother's heart. Running away instead of facing the music. Shaming his family. But that was a lot of years ago. Jason's gone. Laina's dead. I worked hard to put that all behind me and have a life again. But I did it. I kept plugging along. So yes, I'm happy."

"Are you?"

"Yes."

"You know what I think?"

"No." I didn't want to know.

"I'll tell you, Tommy: I don't think I've ever met a man who was so happy, and yet so miserable."

I let that sink in, and it hurt. He was saying my happiness was a facade. Was it? Yes, of course it was. I'd always known that, on some level. And yet I justified it. What else was I supposed to do, when life denied me such fundamental joys as my own wife and son?

I brushed the sawdust off the dashboard and let my eye lose itself in the twisting patterns of the birdseye. "You of all people should know that happiness is hard to come by in this world. Sometimes a little is enough."

He didn't reply. A weighty silence hung between us for several moments. Wade finally broke it with a heavy sigh.

"I didn't just come to tell you about Bailey. We've had a crack in the murder investigation."

"Really?" I wasn't sure I was interested right now.

Wade looked down at his hands and nodded, chewing his lip. "We got the data from Fritz's phone," he said. "There was a message in his voicemail. From Jason."

At the sound of my son's name, a trickle of adrenaline seeped into my bloodstream. I said nothing. Waited for Wade to go on.

"Fritz was going to go to the police. He was going to turn himself in. You know we would have interviewed him for all the details on the burglaries. Jason warned him not to do it. Said he would be here in Lake Geneva in a matter of hours. He left that message the day before Fritz died." Wade paused and brushed a few more grains of sawdust off the workbench. "You realize what this could mean?"

My palms turned cold and clammy. I knew what Wade was saying. The line of thought he was laying down. That Jason could have killed Fritz. I wiped the sweat from my palms off on my work jeans then turned back to the dashboard. I worked the sandpaper carefully around the circular openings where the brass-ringed gauges would go.

"Tommy, I'm thinking about the message left on your window. Do you want to stay with Nancy and me for a few days?" he finally asked. "Until we find Jason?"

"You've been looking for him for seventeen years," I pointed out.

Wade slit his eyes snidely. "He was in Washington D.C. Now he's in Lake Geneva."

That stung, for some reason. To know where Jason had been. It stung that Wade was aware of that information before I was. What stung worst was that I coulda just grabbed a plane ticket for D.C. and paid Jason a visit—if he hadn't been wanted by the police in four counties. I had the sudden impulse to stab a screwdriver into the dashboard, leaving a gouge in the wood. Strange. I'd known since I was a boy that life was unfair. You'd think I was just figuring that out now.

I considered Wade's offer. I knew what it would mean to move in with him and his wife, if only for a few days. It would mean walls full of family photos. Kids dropping off grandkids for the day. Family dinners every so often, three generations seated around the table. It would mean everything I didn't have, but wanted desperately. Everything I'd lost when I lost my son.

I shook my head. "Thanks, Wade. I'll be fine."

"I would feel better if you did," Wade insisted.

And I would feel better if I didn't. "What murderer warns his victims before he kills them?" I pointed out. "Especially if he's really trying to clean house. He'd just up and do it, no preludes. Jason's not after me. Or Roland, for that matter."

Wade eyed me askance. I could see he was grappling with Jason's criminal record versus my vote for his innocence in the current matter. Maybe he was throwing Jason's mental health into the mix, too. Maybe mine. Whatever way I sliced it, it was obvious Wade didn't agree with me.

He sighed. "It's up to you, Tommy. But promise me you'll lock your doors and keep the yard light on."

"Sure," I said.

"And you'll call me if anything else happens."

"Okay."

Wade nodded. "Okay." He stood awkwardly for a moment, hands on his gun belt, thumbs tapping the leather. "Will you think about what I said?"

"About my depression, disillusionment, and state of denial?"

"You know what I mean."

"I think about it all the time."

"Oh. Then I guess I didn't need to say anything."

I laid down the sanding block with an exasperated sigh. "It's okay, Wade. Maybe you had a point."

"Maybe," he agreed. "You take care, Tommy. I'll keep you informed."

"Thanks," I said. But there was no heart in it.

After Wade left, I tried dry-fitting the dashboard into its place in the Cadet. Was it still too snug, or was it just right? I pounded the edges with my fist. It wouldn't go.

Something burned in my chest. Anger. Life was cruel. My only son had grown up to kill a peace officer. Now maybe he'd killed one of his best friends. According to Wade, he was out to kill Roland and me next.

Where had I gone wrong?

## CHAPTER THIRTY-FOUR
## JASON

It was late when he finally arrived in the outskirts of Lake Geneva. He stopped for coffee at a gas station that hadn't existed seventeen years ago. With any luck, the attendant behind the till would be some kid who hadn't existed seventeen years ago. Instead, the pudgy man working the graveyard shift appeared to be in his late thirties. Jason didn't recognize him, though—and hopefully there was no reason for him to recognize the escaped bank burglar and cop killer from Lake Geneva's past. Jason had been tempted to walk into the store wearing shades, but at eleven at night, that would have been a dead giveaway. Instead, he hoped the grungy baseball cap pulled over his wavy brown hair would do.

Fine—his wavy salt-and-pepper hair. Much had changed in seventeen years.

Fritz hadn't returned any of his calls. Now they were all going straight to voicemail. Fritz was probably rethinking his life from a jail cell—and Lake Geneva was the last place on earth Jason should be, unless he was looking forward to joining his buddy behind bars. He quit calling Fritz in case his phone was in police custody. Then he dumped his cell phone in the baggage of a lady waiting for a plane to Fort

Lauderdale and bought a prepaid deal at Walmart as soon as he'd landed in Chicago.

His bad luck always came in spurts. As if it weren't bad enough that his painstakingly concealed past was coming unraveled, all planes out of D.C. had been grounded by thunderstorms. Roads were shut down. He'd told Fritz he'd be in Lake Geneva in a matter of hours. Now here it was, four days later. Four days. And Fritz wasn't answering his phone. Anything could have happened. Jason should be in Canada right now. Or Europe. Anywhere but Lake Geneva.

He set his coffee on the counter and pulled out his wallet.

The attendant folded up the newspaper he'd been browsing and punched his till to life. "Gas?"

"No, just the coffee." His rental car from Chicago had come with a full tank. He, however, needed desperately to refuel. Whatever was awaiting him in Lake Geneva, he was certain it was about to be a long night.

The clerk punched more buttons. "Two fourteen."

Jason's eye glanced across the paper the attendant had been reading. The headline shouted, "BODY RECOVERED FROM LAKE. POLICE SUSPECT FOUL PLAY."

His heart drummed. He knew. Without even needing a name, he just knew. That's why Fritz wasn't returning his calls.

It dawned on him that the attendant was waiting. "Uh ... where can I get a copy of the paper?"

"Over there." He pointed to a low shelf to the left sporting Chicago, Milwaukee, and Madison papers, plus the local *Lake Geneva Regional News*. Jason grabbed the local. The rest he could pick up anywhere to see if the story was spreading. Buying them all at once might look suspicious.

He threw the paper down on the counter beside the coffee. "That, too."

The attendant punched buttons again. "Three twenty-one."

140

Jason bypassed his credit cards and handed the man a five. The name Eric Butler was unknown in Lake Geneva, but after glimpsing that headline, he didn't dare let his alias leave a paper trail in town. He had plenty of cash.

The attendant handed him his change. Without another word, Jason took the paper and the coffee to the car and turned on the engine. He wouldn't risk staying there to read the article. What if the attendant started thinking?

God, he was paranoid.

But paranoia had kept his hide out of prison for seventeen years.

He pulled into a Walmart parking lot—Lake Geneva had a Walmart now? Gees—cut the engine and turned to the newspaper. A body found submerged at the end of the pier at 980 South Lake Shore Drive showed signs of foul play, and police were investigating the case as a homicide. The body had tentatively been identified as forty-one-year-old Fritz Geissler, wanted in several counties on charges of armed robbery, resisting arrest, and the attempted murder of a police officer.

Jason sighed and closed his eyes. At least Fritz's charge was only *attempted* murder. Jason had always been the better hand down at the shooting range. All that practice had paid off. With a murder charge.

Thanks to him, a cop was dead.

He'd dated the guy's kid sister once. In high school. Individual lives in small towns were hopelessly overlapped. The next paragraph in the article proved that point. Fritz's body had been discovered by the Mailboat girl after a mistimed jump that landed her in the lake.

The Mailboat. So his dad had been there when Fritz's body was discovered.

His dad was over seventy years old now, but Jason knew for a fact that he was still driving that old boat. Every now and again, he Googled the Mailboat—and in every newspaper article, every YouTube video, sure enough,

Tommy Thomlin was still at the helm. Once or twice, he'd been pleasantly surprised to see his dad on a national news outlet. The Mailboat was really one-of-a-kind.

And Jason was always relieved to see that his dad looked good. Older. But good. It seemed like nothing ever slowed him down.

Now, sitting in a Walmart parking lot on the edge of town, he felt a pull in his chest. As if he knew his dad were nearby—within a couple of miles. Jason could almost feel his presence. He'd give anything to pull up in front of the old place, walk through the door, and throw his arms around his dad. He fantasized a warm reception.

But it was, of course, a fantasy.

All he'd ever wanted was to make his father proud. Obviously, he'd screwed that up pretty bad. He knew, without needing to be told, that his dad was furious with him.

He scanned the article a second time. Fritz was dead. Why? Jason fought with the notion that the answer was glaringly obvious. Fritz's body had been dumped at the pier at 980 South Lake Shore Drive.

His stomach churned sickeningly. After all these years, were their secrets no longer safe? Chills ran up and down his spine.

He crumpled up the paper into the passenger seat and fired up the engine. He'd lingered too long already. He had to get out of Lake Geneva.

After one stop. Every second in this town was a risk to his life. But this was one stop he would literally die to make. And he knew she'd never tell on him.

# CHAPTER THIRTY-FIVE
## JASON

It was on the road to Milwaukee. A ten-minute drive. Once he got there, he'd take five minutes. Just five minutes.

He found the iron fence and the red brick pillars in the dark. Turned off the highway and drove at a crawl through the graveyard. He knew where to find the Thomlin family plot. He remembered when his grandmother was buried there, and his uncle. He knew where his father would one day be buried. As a matter of fact, there was a spot for him, too. If his dad hadn't sold it out of spite.

He found the area, marked by a mature, spreading pine tree, and parked. For a moment, he sat with his hands in his lap and his window rolled down. It was a warm night. The breeze carried the sound of crickets, and the smell of mowed grass and fresh pine needles. On one side of the gravel road, headstones marched down the hillside toward the highway. On the other side, farmland rolled away into the distance, covered in the tender leaves of young corn stalks, shivering in the breeze.

He'd dreamed of this moment. It was the only tender welcome he could expect in Lake Geneva.

He got out of the car and walked toward a set of headstones. The small headstone in the center was familiar—Grandma Thomlin. He knew the flat stone on the left, too. His uncle. But the modest double headstone on his right was new to him.

His throat choked up as he drew close and dropped to one knee. The finger-like shadows of the pine tree caressed the edges of the granite, milky in the moonlight. He reached out reverently and traced the carved name. ELAINA MARIE THOMLIN.

A fresh wreath of flowers leaned against each headstone. He touched the soft petals. His dad had been here not long ago. There was no one else in the family. Jason was happy to know his father was taking such good care of the graves. But it shouldn't have been his responsibility alone.

Jason should have been there to help him.

He blew a sigh and rested his hand on his mother's headstone. "Hey, Mom. I'm home."

How many times had he walked through the door after school or on college break and said those words? And his mother would wrap her arms around him and kiss him soundly. And she'd pull out the coffee and sit him down and pester him for all the details of his school life—and most especially if there was "anyone special?" There had been a few. But never any who were special enough to bring home to meet his parents.

His dad heard the names of various girls come and go, frowned, and said nothing. But his mother stroked Jason's arm and said the right one would come along. Then she would top off his coffee mug and ask about finals.

She never did come along—the right girl. And under the current circumstances, a long-term relationship was no longer an option. There had been countless one-night stands—and Jason still felt his father frowning, deeper than ever.

He felt him frowning now, condemning him for visiting his mother's grave secretly, in the middle of the night, when he should have been *there* for her during her last illness, like any decent son would have been.

Jason stroked the stone. "I'm sorry, Mom. I really blew it. I guess you shouldn'ta scolded Dad for all those times he took me out to the woodshed. Maybe if he'd switched me one or two more times, I would have turned out right."

He said it in jest. His parents had never used corporal punishment on him. But Jason had always felt the responsibility of living up to his father's expectations. He was the only son. And he'd been a dutiful son, living up to every one of those expectations, even when he was away at college. He made A's in all his classes. He made sure to be named in local newspapers at least once a year, for sports or speech or volunteer work. And to top it all off, he'd been the assistant vice president of a Chicago bank by the time he was twenty-four. Roland Markham had pulled some strings for that to happen, but an assistant vice president he was, plaque and all.

For some reason, it wasn't until after he'd become an adult—and was suffocating under the demand for perfection—that the lid blew off and he rebelled.

In secret.

His parents never knew. They never knew about the break-ins, the heists, the burglaries, the millions, or where the new car came from—until the day he killed a police officer in a gun battle and ran out of town.

Jason sighed. "I really didn't turn out right. I'm sorry. I didn't even remember to bring you flowers."

He reached up to his shirt collar and pulled out a tarnished ball chain. Dangling from the end was a silver ship's helm. He fingered it gently. It had been a gift from his mother when he left for college. Something to remember her and dad by. "So you can carry a piece of us with you always," she said. Maybe it more strongly represented her hope that her husband and her son would one day be closer.

He wanted to stay as long as possible. All night, maybe. Just to relive memories of his mother and talk with her. But he had to move on. There was no safety for him here.

He laid a kiss on his fingertips and transferred it to his mother's name on the headstone. "I love you, Mom." Then he touched his father's name on the other side, already filled out for him but lacking a date. A date he would also miss. He sighed. "I love you, Dad."

He knew his dad wouldn't believe him.

He rose, tucked the ship's helm back inside his shirt, brushed grass and pine needles from his knees, and returned to his car. Turning on the engine, he prepared for the drive to Chicago, and from there, a flight back to D.C. and his job as a politician's assistant. What better place for him—a man running from the law—than to work for a man who made laws?

Just as he approached the brick pillars, a low black car turned off the highway and sped up the road. Who would be in a hurry to get to a graveyard? At this time of night?

Unless they were looking for someone living.

Jason stepped on the gas. The car leapt forward toward the gateway. He could squeeze through just in time ...

The black car charged straight toward him, headlights blinding. They were going to crash head-on.

Jason swerved. The nose of his car buried itself in the iron fence and put out one of its own headlights on the corner of the brickwork. He reversed, ready to shoot through the opening as soon as the other car had careened through. But instead, it fishtailed, blocking the entire opening. The driver leapt out and bore down on Jason's open driver's side window, aiming a gun.

He vaguely recognized the face—though it had aged.

Roland's next-door neighbor. Charles Hart.

## CHAPTER THIRTY-SIX
## JASON

Jason sat at a dining room table; the kind with carved legs as thick as his arms. The vase in the middle was full of lilies; he couldn't tell if they were real or silk, but he thought they were real. The room was half in shadow, where the light from the antique brass ceiling candelabra failed to reach, and the chair was stiff and formal, with velvet seats and little velvet pads embedded in the arms.

Jason had to focus on keeping his hands loose as they rested on the thighs of his jeans. He hoped the sweat under his arms wasn't soaking through his tee shirt. He didn't need Charles to see his fear.

The old man paced the worn wood floor. "So," he said. "What say you to our little plan?"

"Is that the same proposition you made to Fritz?"

"It is."

"And he said no." Jason didn't have to ask. It was a statement. Fritz was dead.

"He said no," Charles agreed. He stopped. His shaved head reflected the light. "And what do *you* say?"

The only muscles Jason let himself flex were those in his jaw. It released the tension, and hopefully made him look stronger than he felt. He lifted his chin. "No. I won't be a part of your plan. I won't be a party to murder."

Charles chuckled, his shoulders heaving. "Murder, Jason?"

He felt his temples flushing. The cop. The dead cop. Seventeen years ago. That man's ghost had followed him around every day of his life, asking him, *Why did you kill me?*

"It wasn't murder," Jason said. "I never meant to kill anyone."

"And yet you have it in you."

"Bobby—"

"Bobby didn't blanch. He was the first to pull a gun that night. You know better than I do; you were there. He would have killed his own father, had he seen a need. He would have killed you, when it comes right down to it."

Jason shook his head. "No."

"Oh, yes, he would have. He and you and I, that's what we all have in common. We don't value a friend so well that we couldn't send them beyond the land of the living, if we saw a need."

He turned to a massive wooden hutch, gloaming with silver, and pulled open a drawer. Wood groaned against wood. He turned around again, gripping a long carving knife.

A shudder raced down Jason's spine and fresh sweat broke out. Out of the corners of his eyes, he looked for something he could use to defend himself. Barring anything else, he'd use the fancy wooden chair he sat in as a shield. He was younger than Charles. He could fend off an attack.

Charles balanced the blade on his palm. "Do you see this knife?"

"Yes," Jason answered, moving nothing but his mouth. Keeping his eyes glued on Charles.

"Fritz was *stabbed* with a knife." He laid a gruesome emphasis on the word *stabbed*. "But that's not how we killed him."

He paced toward Jason. Slow. Real slow. Jason could almost sense his every move before he made it. But he knew that when the man made his attack, it would be quick. Out of the blue. Jason watched him as he stood beside his chair.

"No," Charles went on. "We strapped him to a pier post by a rope around his neck and choked him until he died." Charles leaned over, bracing his fist with the knife in it on the table in front of them. He whispered thickly in Jason's ear. "I. Killed. Fritz."

When Jason and Bobby and Fritz were boys, they had called Roland's neighbor "Uncle Charles," but for the life of him, he didn't know why. He wasn't much of an uncle. They used to make fun of him because he was so stiff, like an old-fashioned butler. They would hide under the long, draping cloth of the dining room table at the Markham house and wait for Charles to sit down. Then they'd tuck daisies in the laces of his patent leather shoes and cover their mouths so they wouldn't giggle.

Charles had never appreciated the joke.

Jason tried to picture the seventy-year-old man wrestling Fritz hand-to-hand and choking him to death. He couldn't do it. Something was missing.

"You killed Fritz? Or you paid someone to do it?"

"It's all the same. I was there. I gave the command. You see, Jason, some things are more important than old friendships. You have a very simple choice to make. Join me ..." He paused and eyed the carving knife. "... or join Fritz. So? What will you have?"

The sweat poured down Jason's back. He eyed the knife and recalled that Charles also had a gun still tucked inside his belt. For a moment, he pictured himself back in the Walmart parking lot, reading about Fritz's death. He pictured his own name in black-and-white in next week's issue.

In the end, it was a simple choice.

"What do I need to do?" he asked.

## CHAPTER THIRTY-SEVEN
## RYAN

Lucky dog that I was, I'd picked up a double shift. One of the other guys had called in sick, and like a sucker, I'd raised my hand. At least I got to sit in a patrol car tonight. My sore backside thanked me. Aside from conducting interviews on Bailey's case, for which I used a patrol car, I was stuck on a bike. The last time I'd clocked that many hours on a bike seat, the ink was still drying on my college diploma. I was getting too old for these kinds of shenanigans.

The bad thing about night patrol is that, if you don't find something to keep yourself busy, you start to think too much. And I had plenty to think about. Bailey, for one. It irked me that all my interviews had turned up nothing—as if her black eye had come out of nowhere. It irked me worse that Bailey wouldn't say a word against whoever was hurting her. A classic case of a victim protecting her abuser out of fear, or even a misplaced sense of loyalty. But Bailey just seemed too intelligent to be loyal to someone who was punching her.

I had the distinct notion that a major piece of that puzzle was still missing.

Less mystifying was Monica. I knew why she hated me—and she had every right to. If I'd known she was back in Lake Geneva again, I never would have come home.

Home? The word struck me as unusual. Was there any place on the face of this earth that I considered to be home? If so, why did I keep pulling up my roots and moving on? Why was I never able to settle down with one woman? Why was I so... restless?

I'd been asking myself this question for a year—ever since my last breakup. Sad that I could number my breakups like so many dozens of eggs. I moved from one city to the next, one woman to the next.

What was I looking for?

I had the rest of a long night open for figuring it out.

# CHAPTER THIRTY-EIGHT
## JASON

Jason hung by his fingertips from the window, contemplating just how high two stories really was and wondering if this would in any way reawaken the high school football injury to his knee. But he didn't really have a choice. Certainly not at this point, dangling full-length out a bedroom window.

With a whispered, "Go, Badgers," he let go and felt his stomach take wings as he plummeted. He hit the ground with a roll and came up clutching his knee. His dad was right. He should have joined the baseball team instead.

They were partners now, Jason and Charles. Just as Jason and Bobby had been partners so many years ago. It was as if the gang had risen again out of the ashes—defeated. Broken. Scattered. Reborn now. And playing a far more dangerous game.

Or so Charles believed. Jason was a little surprised how gullible Charles had proven. Granted, the old man had locked Jason into his bedroom for the night, but still. That was better than having a knife sliced across his throat. This way, he had time to escape.

Which was exactly what he was doing.

A light flicked on in a window to his left. Jason whispered a four-letter word, scrambled to his feet, and ducked around the corner of the house. Up close and personal with a prickly arborvitae bush, he froze and listened.

Should he take one of Charles's cars, like he'd planned? Or was he out of time? Should he sneak away on foot and pick up the next car he found?

Charles's cars had one benefit—besides built-in massage in leather seats. Charles wasn't likely to report the theft.

When nothing stirred in either the house or the yard, Jason parted with the arborvitae and dashed across the driveway, limping on his knee. He reached the three-stall garage, ducked down in a shadowy corner, and waited. Still no sign of movement.

He pushed open the side door to the garage silently. He had a choice between a Lamborghini, a Ferrari, and a Mercedes. He gave a low whistle. Charles had good taste in horsepower.

All he needed was a screwdriver and wire cutters. Metal cabinets lined the walls of the garage. Jason pulled them open one-by-one. They were largely empty, except for the odd bit of rope and plenty of car wax and chamois. Apparently Charles was the type to putter on the exterior rather than under the hood.

He finally found a small tool box. It looked brand new and completely unused. The screwdriver was in the top tray. Wire cutters were in the second drawer.

He chose the Lamborghini for no other reason than that it was the closest to him. Finding the door unlocked, he sprawled on the driver's seat and took the screws out of the panel under the steering wheel. His pounding heart told him to rush, but his head told him to take it slow and quiet. He'd be out of there in a matter of moments. He snipped four wires and twisted them together in twos. Suddenly, the engine was purring. Jason released held breath. He was free.

The garage lights flicked on. "Good morning, Jason."

Jason looked up. Charles stood by the door in a velvet bathrobe tied over pajama pants. He had fuzzy slippers on his feet and a gun in his hand.

Jason slammed the driver's door shut and put the Lamborghini in reverse. He didn't have to worry anymore about getting the garage door open quietly.

He smashed right through it.

Wood splintered in every direction. He backed over the broken pieces and braked just shy of crashing into a tree.

Charles stood in the midst of the rubble, raised his arm straight out, and fired.

Jason ducked. He wasn't sure where the bullet hit the car, but it made a sound like a giant bug going *splat* at highway speed.

He put the car in drive, twisted the wheel, and peeled out of the driveway. More gunshots followed him, but none hit. He turned onto South Lake Shore Drive and floored the gas. The Lambo jumped forward so fast, Jason thought he'd left his stomach behind.

The game wasn't over yet. Charles would be grabbing his keys to one of the other cars and the chase would be on.

He couldn't go straight to his dad's house. He couldn't bring a gun battle to his door. A one-sided gun battle, at that. For now, he was going to have to disappear. The best place for him when daylight came would be a large city where he could blend in. Milwaukee was only an hour away.

Headlights appeared in his rear view mirror.

Jason set his jaw. Time to see what this engine could do.

## CHAPTER THIRTY-NINE
## RYAN

Bailey and Monica ... Monica and Bailey ...

As I sat in my patrol car yawning, it dawned on me that taking the double shift was just the most recent in a long string of bad decisions—my specialty. Between questioning life choices, I counted down the hours. Tonight was particularly quiet.

Quiet, until I heard the engines roaring. Moments later, a silver Lamborghini ripped past me with a red Ferrari on its tail. I popped my eyebrows.

This was the kind of chase cops dreamed of.

I thumped the dash on my Dodge Charger. "You up for this, girl?"

Flicking on the lights and sirens, I hit the gas, deciding to believe that my cruiser was on a par with any millionaire's toy. My tires squealed as I pulled in behind them.

"Forty-four thirty-seven to LGPD," I said into my radio. "Street race heading north on South Lake Shore Drive. I'm in pursuit of a silver Lamborghini and a red Ferrari."

"Ten-four, 4437."

"Forty-four sixteen to 4437, I'm on Edwards Boulevard heading north to Main Street. I'll back you up."

I clicked the button on the mic again. "Ten-four." Mike Schultz—better known as 4416 on the air—was my partner in crime-fighting for the night. He was driving parallel to me, but about a mile to my right.

The super cars were headed north towards downtown and driving like bats out of hell.

I grinned smolderingly. If they were the bats, I was the Devil.

## CHAPTER FORTY
### JASON

At the sight of flashing red and blue lights in his rear-view mirror, Jason's heart leapt into his throat. If he'd thought there was nothing worse than being chased by Fritz's murderer, he was wrong. Being chased by Fritz's murderer *and* the cops was worse. Way worse. He'd never felt so cornered in his life, like a mouse caught between an owl and a cat.

The road curved ahead. He was supposed to take the bend, deep into downtown toward the lakefront and the piers. Another street continued in a straight line and would take him directly to Main Street and from there to the freeway to Milwaukee. But the street was a one-way—the wrong way—and there was a car coming toward him.

Really? Who would be out driving in a small town at this time of night? Besides him, a cop, and a killer.

Jason glanced at the Ferrari and the cruiser in his rear-view mirror and took the one-way.

## CHAPTER FORTY-ONE
## RYAN

These people were manic.

The driver of the Lambo went straight for the one-way, never mind there was a car coming right at him. He hit the horn. The other car swerved sideways, putting two wheels on the curb. The Lamborghini shot past, followed by the Ferrari.

I debated a moment, then followed. Like I said, I was the Devil. And I wasn't about to let two super cars get the best of me and my Dodge.

"They're headed north up the one-way," I reported into the radio. "Toward Main Street." That was a T-intersection. They could go east or they could go west. I laid my money on east. They would want to head for the freeway and put some real power into their chase.

The Lamborghini made a screeching right-hand turn onto Main Street. I may or may not have pounded the steering wheel and yelled a victory cry. My prediction was right. The Ferrari followed around the sharp corner, and I brought up the rear, gripping the wheel with both hands. My gun dug into my hip as I leaned into the turn. The cruiser fish-tailed, but I pulled out of it—

And was crushed to see how far the super cars had shot ahead of me. Apparently, my cruiser wasn't quite on a par with a millionaire's toy. I'll admit to being pretty heart-broken. In my mind, I'd seen myself pull alongside the Ferrari and give the young punk driver a cool scowl that would send him to the curb like a pup with his tail between his legs. The reality was that both the Ferrari and the Lamborghini had stepped on the gas as soon as they'd come out of the turn, and now they were disappearing into the distance.

"Forty-four sixteen, where are you?" I asked of the radio mic.

"I just turned onto Main Street, heading west," Schultz replied.

"Stay where you are and lay down some stop sticks," I told him. Then I said the words that broke my heart. "I can't keep up with them." The Lambo was off and running and we'd be lucky if we caught the Ferrari. If I'd ever wondered which car was faster, I now knew. The Ferrari was eating the Lambo's dust. "Hurry up or we'll never catch them."

"Ten-four," Schultz replied.

Even from my distance, the roar of the sports cars rattled my chest. They flashed in and out of the pools of light cast by the street lamps. Where was Schultz? I scanned the street and finally spotted another cruiser several blocks ahead of me, and Schultz flipping open the trunk.

The Lambo shot past him.

I hit the steering wheel again and cussed Schultz out. I'll admit to being a sore loser. I really wanted to catch that Lamborghini.

"Forty-four thirty-seven to LGPD," I called in to the dispatcher. "Silver Lamborghini passed my backup before stop sticks could be deployed. It's heading east toward the junction of 50 and 12. Is HP nearby?"

The radio crackled. "LGPD to 4437, ten-four. HP will continue pursuit of the Lamborghini. Do you have a license plate number?"

I frowned at my radio. No, I didn't have a license plate number. If the highway patrol couldn't find the only speeding silver Lamborghini on the road at one in the morning, I sure enough couldn't help them. I simply said, "Negative," into the microphone and left it at that.

Up ahead, Schultz emerged from the trunk of his car with a series of interlinked sticks—triangular with red decals, as if the pixie-high stick could talk a speeding car into halting merely by its color similarity to a stop sign. He glanced down the street and saw his remaining quarry fast approaching. I've never seen a stop stick deployed so fast. As if throwing a curling stone, he shoved the sticks across the road in the path of the oncoming vehicle and jogged backwards out of the way.

A heavy thump filled my ears as the Ferrari rolled over the projecting spikes.

A car can go surprisingly far on flat tires. I've seen subjects who refused to stop until miles later when the rims were striking sparks on the road and setting the remaining rubber on fire.

I smacked my lips, looking forward to roasting marshmallows over a Ferrari.

But to my surprise, the sports car wobbled back and forth before careening to an ungraceful stop in the middle of the sidewalk.

I stomped on the break. My cruiser screeched to a halt and I smelled burning rubber. Schultz pulled up alongside me. He sprang out of his car, drew his weapon, and pointed it at the driver in a two-handed grip.

I radioed in our exact location. Then I thumbed my mic and flipped a switch. "Driver of the red Ferrari," I said, my voice booming through the street, "roll down your window and drop your keys out of your car." I tried to keep the stress out of my voice. It had a bad habit of cracking like a teenage boy's when my adrenaline was up. Somebody who ran from the police probably had a reason to run. A reason to risk his own life, and ours, and the lives of bystanders in a high-speed chase. That was why Schultz had his gun drawn. Why we would land this fish slowly and carefully. Why we would make him throw his keys out first, then exit the car with his hands up, then walk towards us backwards where we would handcuff and frisk him.

Or so the script was written at the police academy.

The driver's side door of the Ferrari burst open and an old man leapt out, his bald head as hot as an oven. He shouted something I couldn't make out.

I cussed under my breath and threw open my door, grabbing my gun in one hurried movement. I gripped the weapon in both hands and pointed it at the driver. "Stop and put your hands up!" I commanded.

He ignored me, gesturing wildly. "Do you know who you've just let get away?" he yelled. "Jason Thomlin!"

## CHAPTER FORTY-TWO
## JASON

They were gone. The flashing lights. Gone. Jason checked about six times before he began to believe it. Charles was gone, too. He was home free.

For a moment.

Seconds after he'd turned onto the freeway, more lights appeared, swirling in his rear view mirror. His heart drummed again.

Then he remembered he was driving a Lamborghini.

And the road was completely open.

With a steadying sigh that puffed his cheeks, he pressed the accelerator flat to the floor.

Moments later, the police cars vanished behind him. For good.

Now to hide in Milwaukee—and find out just how much hot water he was in.

## CHAPTER FORTY-THREE
## RYAN

I stared without blinking at the bald-headed man I'd just pulled over. Part of my brain was still trying to figure out what an old man was doing street racing in a bathrobe and fuzzy slippers. Another part was trying to fathom if Jason Thomlin—the killer Monica was trying to catch—could really be escaping in that blasted silver Lamborghini. What little brain capacity I had left was focused on making this old man comply with orders. Fleeing from police in a vehicle was a felony, and this guy was headed for prison.

"Stop where you are and put your hands up!" I said again.

"You're letting a killer get away!" the man yelled. "He tried to break into Roland Markham's house. I scared him off. Quit wasting your time with me!"

My mind scrambled to process the conflicting information. This guy claimed he was trying to help us?

"Brandt!" Schultz shouted. "He has something in his right pocket. Watch it!"

I glanced at the square patch pocket. It drooped under the weight of something heavy.

First things first. Get the cuffs on him. Sort the rest out later.

"Sir," I shouted clearly and firmly, "put your hands on your head. Do it now."

He paused just a beat too long.

Then he thrust his hand into his pocket and withdrew a small revolver. The next thing I knew, he was storming toward me, pointing the revolver at my chest and pulling the trigger. Repeatedly.

At the end of the day, a car door doesn't actually stop a bullet. The engine block is the only part of a car that will absorb those bits of flying lead. I wasn't behind the engine block. The bullets hit me like a hammer. *Boom. Boom. Boom.*

I landed flat on my back on the pavement, staring up into a street lamp.

More gunshots. I couldn't see Schultz, but I knew at least half the bullets now flying were his. "Shots fired! Officer down!" he yelled during a lull in the gunfire.

Officer down.

Me.

I was down. I'd been shot. I waited for the white-hot pain to hit. Instead, I felt like I'd been punched in the chest with a bowling ball. I'd never felt so exposed in my life, lying belly-up in the middle of a barren street with shots zipping back and forth around me.

I hadn't signed up for this when I volunteered to take a double shift.

Was this it? End of watch for Ryan Brandt? Time slowed, and I thought I heard bagpipes skirling the tune of "Amazing Grace" and rifles firing the twenty-one gun salute. I saw burly men in dress uniform crying over my flag-draped casket while reporters' cameras flashed at my funeral. I heard tender words spoken ...

And then, in my imagination, Chief Wade Erickson stuttered and said apologetically, "Actually, there's not a lot I can think to say about Ryan. He didn't do all that much."

And in that moment, out of disgust in myself, I decided not to die.

With a groan, I grabbed my gun out of my holster and leaned on my elbow. It wasn't the best shooting form, but it felt better than lying there like roadkill. I squeezed off a couple shots.

The man in the velvet bathrobe and fuzzy slippers fired back, but his revolver clicked emptily. With a panicked expression, he ducked back into the driver's seat and slammed the door. He drove over the sidewalk and the lawn next to it, leaving bits of grass and dirt flying through the air.

Seconds later, he was gone.

Schultz was yelling into his radio for an ambulance.

I tried to sit up, but pain pounded through my chest and I dropped back down onto my back.

"Brandt!" Schultz yelled, falling to his knees beside me. "Where are you hit?"

"My chest," I wheezed.

He ripped open my shirt. A severed button rolled to a stop next to my ear. I waited for him to tell me it was bad.

Schultz laughed. "God, Brandt. Look at you. There's three bullets stuck in your vest."

My vest? Much as I hated the hot, heavy thing, I'd forgotten I was wearing it.

Thank God I was.

I was nearly overtaken by a strong need to cry. Shock. Adrenaline. Relief. Instead, I barked at Schultz, "Take the damn thing off. I can hardly breathe."

He ripped open the Velcro straps and removed the chest plate. I took a deep breath that ached in every rib.

"You're lucky, Ryan," Mike said.

I was. But why? Why had I been spared tonight? I could just as easily have been shot in the head. Or severed a major artery in a limb and bled out before it was all over.

But I hadn't. It wasn't like the world would stop revolving without me.

*Actually, there's not a lot I can think to say about Ryan,* Wade's imagined voice rolled through my head again. *He didn't do all that much.*

## CHAPTER FORTY-FOUR
## MONICA

Main Street was flashing like Vegas when I arrived. My mind was spinning, and it had little to do with being rousted out of bed in the middle of the night. Ryan had been shot. Or shot at. I still wasn't clear on his condition. Of course, by the time I got there, he and the ambulance were already gone.

I was shaking, and I really wasn't sure why.

"Detective!" Mike Schultz waved me down from near the yellow tape. Lacking any other direction to go, I approached him.

"What happened?" I asked. What I really meant was, "How's Brandt?" but everyone knew I hated him. So I didn't say that.

Schultz took a deep breath and let it all out slowly. I could tell he was still shaken. "It was crazy," he said. "It just came out of nowhere."

He unfolded the story to me, detail-by-detail, and I nodded intelligently. I waited patiently until he got to the part where he took off Brandt's shirt and found the bullets lodged in his vest.

Ryan was all right.

The snarky side of me said I didn't care. I told the snarky side of me to shut the hell up. Dammit, yes, I cared.

Nobody was allowed to beat up Ryan but me. As his ex-wife, I reserved those privileges for myself.

And by God, I would skin Charles Hart alive when I found him.

Hart. I could hardly believe it. The silent next-door neighbor. What had possessed him to shoot an officer? It suddenly dawned on me that I knew a lot less about this case than I thought. How did Hart fit in? Why was he carrying the gun, and why would he rather attempt to murder an officer than hand that gun over?

Maybe because the story he'd given wasn't true.

Had Hart actually been chasing Jason Thomlin? If that part was true, then who was really cleaning house? Jason ... or Charles? What kind of ties might Charles have to the old burglary ring?

My mind buzzed with questions, and I hadn't had any coffee yet to help me sort them out.

But Ryan was all right. That much I could process.

## CHAPTER FORTY-FIVE
## BAILEY

The sun hadn't peeked over the top of the Riviera yet, and it was almost nippy on board the Mailboat while it sat in the shadow of the building. Today, I was glad for the long sleeves. Yep, I was still wearing them.

Kneeling on the bow of the boat, I squirted the windshield with cleaner and scrubbed it down with a wad of paper towel. I could see Tommy through the glass, sorting through newspapers and writing the names of the recipients across the top. I was pretty sure he had the names down, in order, by memory, even though a cheat sheet sat nearby. I needed the cheat sheet sometimes. He never did.

We were practically facing each other through the glass, but I didn't look at him and he didn't look at me. In fact, aside from a quick "good morning" nearly an hour ago, we hadn't spoken to each other.

It was like somebody had pointed the wrong ends of two magnets at each other and we were both pushing each other away.

I hated it. And I didn't know why he was so talkative yesterday and so silent today. I wracked my brain for whatever I'd done wrong. He knew I was lying to him about my bruises. Maybe that's why he was mad at me.

For the hundred gazillionth time, I considered telling him why I didn't want to move to another foster home. But every time I thought I was about to open my mouth, I realized that saying nothing was just so much easier, and a flood of relief would wash over me, and I would go back to scrubbing windows.

Besides, there was only one home I really wanted to go to. One person I wanted to call my foster dad. Or maybe my grandpa. And I knew I would never find the courage to say it out loud.

There was only one person I wanted to adopt me. Tommy.

So I dreamed. Dreams were happy. Dreams were safe. There was no risk of rejection in dreams.

People didn't abandon me in my dreams.

## CHAPTER FORTY-SIX
### TOMMY

I glanced at Bailey when I was sure she wasn't looking. She seemed to be avoiding me. Good.

I hated myself for feeling like that.

Yesterday morning, when I'd sat her down for our little talk, I had been on the verge of telling her to come to me if she needed anything. And at the last moment, I bailed out. Told her to go to her social worker instead.

Why had I done that?

Because Wade was right. I held everyone at the end of a stick. I didn't want to be there for anyone. I'd completely failed at fathering my own child. Jason had abandoned me.

Maybe that was the root of it all. I was afraid of being abandoned again. Of adoring Bailey like a father ... only to have her break my heart someday. After all, there were no guarantees in life.

## CHAPTER FORTY-SEVEN
## MONICA

I had the seats laid down in the back of my unmarked SUV and sat on the floor with my legs criss-cross. I was thinking about a cramp in my back and chewing on a hangnail. I'd been here all day and was bored out of my wits. Not to mention exhausted from having been up half the night. Coffee would have been great, but I hated peeing into a cup any more than I had to. And besides, coffee would mean leaving my post.

I cussed out Lehman for landing the fun job of interviewing Hart's friends and family while I sat in my car sweltering. How had I drawn the short straw?

Charles Hart hadn't come home yet. Or maybe he'd gotten here before me and was hiding in the house. There was a Mercedes sitting in the garage—I peeked—but no sign of the Ferrari. I couldn't tell if he was here or wasn't. He could have switched cars or even gotten here on foot.

Also notable was the broken garage door. It lay in countless splinters all over the driveway, as if someone had driven right through it. I spent a good amount of time contemplating that broken garage door and what it could mean. The door next to it stood open in the normal way.

I had an equally good view of Roland Markham's house and yard. It was just as damn quiet as Hart's place.

It didn't matter anymore.

We had an arrest warrant. We were going in.

I heard what sounded like a diesel engine rumbling down the street and looked up. Sure enough, a hulking truck appeared, olive drab in color, traveling at a clip. I imagined the fully-geared tactical team bouncing around inside, rifles pointed at the floor. They would be pumped and ready for action, and making a pact to watch out for each other. After all, this man had tried to murder one of our own.

One of *my* own. My ex.

The truck jerked to a halt several yards away from the house. Everything that happened next happened in a hurry. Men in drab-colored uniforms poured out the doors like clowns-from-hell jumping out of a car. They kept coming, a dozen of them. Their heads were clad in Kevlar helmets. Vests with the power to stop a rifle bullet hung heavily off their shoulders, the word *SWAT* emblazoned across their backs. The man in the lead carried a shield. The next, a battering ram the length of his arm. Another had a flashbang that just fit in his hand. The rest were bristling with assault rifles.

They swarmed at the door—a solid, blood red slab of wood with fancy stained-glass sidelights. One man pounded on the door.

"Police! Arrest warrant! Police! Arrest warrant!"

And that was all the warning Hart got. The team member with the battering ram needed only one swing to pop open the door. He had good form, I noted, rotating at the hips and using his whole body to put enough force into the ram. The next officer tossed in the flashbang and everyone stood back, pressing their bodies against the exterior wall.

The explosion was bright white. Smoke billowed out of the door. Bits of plaster even dropped down from the ceiling.

With the shield-bearer leading the way, the team flowed into the house.

And now I was blind, and wondering what they were finding. If Hart was home. If he still had that revolver. If I was about to hear gunshots, or somebody screaming, "Officer down!"

I chewed on that hangnail until I ripped it out and left a painful spot of blood. I cussed. Chewing on hangnails never turns out as intended.

My cell phone rang in my pocket. I nearly leapt out of my skin. I grabbed my phone and looked at the display. It was Joe Trevorly, the SWAT team leader. I picked up.

"Detective Steele."

"I assume that's your car across the street?"

"Yep. I've been here all goddamn day."

"Sorry to disappoint. The house and garage are clear."

Damn. All that waiting for nothing.

"Find anything interesting yet?"

"Yes. Come on in and I'll show you."

"Be right there."

I thanked whatever deity was in charge of the universe as I hung up and stretched my aching legs. I had begun to picture the rest of my life passing slowly in the back of an SUV. Hopping out one of the back doors, I realized just how bad I had to pee. That was just going to have to wait.

I crossed the street and the yard, climbed the front steps, and entered the home. Trevorly was standing on the opposite side of the broken plaster from the flashbang, the shape of his body disguised by bulky armor, his assault rifle pointed at the ground.

"Come upstairs," he said.

He led me up an oak staircase, stained a dark brown and covered in red velvety carpet. However many searches I'd been on, and despite the warrant permitting us to legally be there, I'd never lost that weird feeling you get when walking through somebody else's home when they're not there. It gets even weirder when all your compadres are bristling with firearms.

At the top landing, Trevorly pointed toward a door with a broken jamb. It opened into a bedroom. The battering ram sat on the floor nearby.

"That door was locked," Trevorly said as he entered the room.

I followed him. He pointed out a window, standing open, with the screen removed and sitting on the floor.

"That's the way we found this window," he said. "What do you make of it?"

"Looks like somebody climbed out," I said. "But nobody left the house while I was running surveillance. Not before you guys came, not after. I had a good view of this side of the house."

I leaned out the window, careful not to touch the frame. There was nothing to climb down. No lattice. No drain pipe. Nothing but a straight drop into a flower bed. I would have to check that for impressions.

I could think of a few scenarios that would explain what I was seeing. Hart might have set the room up to look like an escape. But why? He might have in fact taken his leave at some point via this window. But again, why? And when? It would have to have been before he'd been stopped for the street race. His house had been under constant surveillance since then.

Or someone might in fact have been locked inside this room and escaped. That same someone might have entered the garage and stolen a silver Lamborghini. Maybe led Hart and later Brandt on a street race through Lake Geneva.

Of all the scenarios, I placed my bet on this one. It fit. Except for one nagging question.

What did Hart have against Jason?

## CHAPTER FORTY-EIGHT
## MONICA

Roland Markham stared out his living room window across the lake, his arms crossed and his hand covering his mouth. The room was so tense and quiet, I could hear the soft ticking of the mantle clock.

"Yes," he finally said.

"Yes what?" I asked.

Markham sighed heavily. "Yes, I know why Charles might—*might,* mind you—be inclined to cause harm to Jason. And Fritz, for that matter."

I lifted my eyebrows.

Markham clasped his hands behind his back and paced. When that wasn't good enough, he sank into the chair across from me and ran his hand through his messy hair.

"Charles is in love with me."

Well, that was no big surprise. "What's that got to do with Jason and Fritz?" I asked.

Markham gently pounded the arm of his chair with his fist. "You must understand, I've said things now and again. Things about those two young men. My son was a good man, until he fell in with them. They corrupted him."

Really? That was an interesting perspective. From my research on the burglary ring, I gathered that Bobby Markham had been the leader. He was the one who had triggered the gun battle, too. If anyone had been doing the leading astray, it was probably Bobby. But I didn't say anything. This was the moment to let Roland talk.

"Charles knows I blame Jason and Fritz," he said. The sunlight had caught his eyes, turning them translucent gray. They matched his hair. "If not for those two boys, my son would still be alive."

He sighed deeply and gazed away toward the window again. "It's hard for me to talk about this. I was raised in another era, you know. No one talked about these things. Charles is a good neighbor and friend. Has been for decades. But I don't feel ... *that way* toward him. I never have. But Charles has told me ... he's told me there's nothing he wouldn't do for me."

The old man chewed his lip. Finally, he said softly, "He knows how much I loved my son."

I tried to pull together the various parts of what Markham was telling me. "So you're saying ... he might have extracted revenge on Jason and Fritz for you? To win your devotion, so to speak?"

Markham didn't reply. But his jaw and his eyebrows were both flexing. He finally looked me in the eye. His were broken and sad, maybe even on the verge of tears.

"He said he would."

## CHAPTER FORTY-NINE
## TOMMY

I dipped a clean cloth into a can of stain and rubbed it across the birdseye maple. The subtle patterns drank up the color and suddenly sprang to life. Ordinarily, the process of watching the patterns unfold would have filled me with satisfied fascination. Tonight, it didn't.

Bailey was weighing on my mind constantly. Maybe Wade was right; I had more sons and daughters than any other man he knew. Sons and daughters like Monica and Ryan had once been. But I'd turned my back on them all. I'd abandoned them when my only birth son had abandoned me. And now I was watching a new crop of kids grow up—kids like Bailey and Noah, whom I hardly knew.

Try as I might, I just wasn't sure how to reverse the process.

But they weren't my responsibility, anyway. They all had families of their own and didn't need me.

All of them except for Bailey.

The staining was done. I balled up the spent rag in my hand and leaned my fists on the counter. I breathed in the aroma of wood stain and sawdust and let it out slowly.

How could a man who raised a killer be any kind of a good influence on the next generation?

I pulled off my glasses and rubbed my eyes, hoping to dissipate the ache that was growing in my forehead. Could I say I knew the kids at the cruise line at all, when I hadn't even known my own son? Why let anyone near when the people closest to you had the most power to hurt you? To break your heart and turn on you?

I threw the rag into the garbage and tamped the lid down on the can of stain. The dashboard would get two more coats, followed by a high-gloss finish. Then I could install it with the brass trim and the gauges.

I turned out the lights, locked the door, and crossed the yard to the house. As per my promise to Wade, I'd left the porch light on. But the yellow glow faded as it stretched across the lawn.

Something rustled in the grass by the lilac hedge. I stopped and looked, but the yard near the alley was dark. Yet I couldn't shake the feeling that something was out-of-place in the shadow between the hedge and the little gray garden shed. I squinted and stepped closer.

The outline of a tall man slowly separated from the darkness.

The hair on the back of my neck bristled. "Get out here where I can see you," I barked.

The man hesitated. Then slid into the light.

My heart stopped and my mouth went dry.

"Hey, Dad."

All I could do was stare, every muscle in my body vibrating.

"I guess you weren't expecting to see me."

I shook my head.

Jason took another tentative step into the center of the yard. "I'm sorry I startled you."

"What are you doing here?" I hoped the intensity of my voice would warn him from coming any closer. It worked. He stopped.

"I gotta tell you something."

"Yeah, I should think so. Where exactly did you wanna start?"

"Look, I don't have much time—"

"True. I'm giving you exactly five minutes." I pulled my cell phone out of my pocket. "And then I'm calling Wade."

Jason held up his hands. "Don't do that. Please, not yet."

"Start explaining, Jason." The volume of my voice surprised even me. I felt the muscles in my neck straining. "Where have you been? How could you do this to me? To your mother? Do you have any idea how you broke her heart? How she cried herself to sleep every night for five years until she died? Did you even know she was dead?"

"I ran across her obituary."

"You ran across her obituary. When you should have been *there* for her. I raised you better than this, Jason. I'm ashamed of you."

"I know. Dad, I'm sorry. I want to talk this all through with you. Later. If we get the chance."

"I've been waiting seventeen years for you to explain to me how any son of mine, with a respectable career and a great life, could have turned to petty theft."

"Something's about to happen."

"*How*, Jason? You tell me, how? How did Bobby get you mixed up in this?"

Jason sighed and glanced away. "It wasn't Bobby. It was a friend of his. A girl he knew. He introduced us, and we started going together. When Bobby started getting in trouble, I backed off from him. But he and Kalli were still friends. And one day, she told me about this big idea he had, and ... I don't know. Somehow she talked me into helping a little. And then all of a sudden, I was helping a lot. And then I was sunk too deep to go back."

I paused. Something Jason had said. "What was her name?"

"Kalli. Kalli Johnson."

"With a *k*?"

"Yeah."

A sick, sinking feeling crept through my stomach, mixed with a shot of adrenalin. Kalli Johnson. With a *k*. "You ... you were going out with her?"

"I was."

Seventeen years ago. Bailey was sixteen. Add in a nine-month pregnancy. It fit. "How come I never heard about this girl?"

Jason smiled wanly. "She wasn't really your type."

From what Bailey said ... that was an understatement. "Then what were you doing with her?"

Jason shrugged. "I don't know. I wanted to do something reckless for once. I was tired of dressing to impress. Of impressing you. I wanted to live life a little dangerously for a while."

I smiled smugly. "Did you get your fill of that yet?"

He met my gaze with honesty and regret. "Yeah, I did. I've wanted to tell you for a long time now: I'm sorry."

I glared at him, the disgust building to a boiling point at an all-time high. Eleven years, Bailey had been in foster care. Practically her whole life. And now her foster parent was sending her to work every morning with bruises on her arms and a black eye.

"You're not nearly sorry enough, Jason."

"I don't suppose I can ever convince you, can I?"

I shook my head. "No. Tell me—this Kalli girl. You were intimate with her, weren't you?"

He held up his hands. "I know you don't approve of that sort of thing—"

"So you were?"

He let his arms hang by his sides. "Yes."

I felt sick. Everything was matching up all too well. "Do you know what became of her?"

He shrugged. "I ran across her obituary, too."

I smiled mirthlessly. "You have a great track record of being there for the people you pretend to love."

Jason hung his head.

My voice shook with emotion as I added, "Especially your daughter."

He snapped back to attention, his mouth slack.

"What? You didn't even know Kalli had a baby? She did. A girl. Her name's Bailey. She's sixteen years old now. Her mom went to prison for drug charges when Bailey was five. She's been in foster care ever since then. Never had a family of her own, or even knew who you were. Whoever the thug is that she's with now, he sends her out in the mornings with bruises on her face and welts on her arms."

Jason slit his eyes. "How do you know all this?" he asked in a tense whisper.

"Because she's my mail girl." I licked my dry lips. "She's my granddaughter." I said the last part in a lower tone—to myself, not to Jason.

Bailey was mine. The thought twisted my gut with fear. The last thing in the world I wanted. Another child. Another child to ruin and send out into the world to wreak havoc. Another child who could break my heart. My knees suddenly felt like water.

"Oh my god," Jason breathed.

That pretty well wrapped up my own sentiment, too.

"Jason. Leave."

"Dad, I'm sorry."

I glared at him. "You disgust me. There's nothing you can say to excuse yourself."

"I know that. But I came here to tell you something. You have to pass it on to Wade."

I shook my head. "I'm not running errands for you. If you have something to tell Wade, you can tell him yourself."

"I can't. Hear me out."

I pointed a finger at him. "No, you hear *me* out. Do the right thing for once, Jason. I want you to drive downtown, march into that police station, and turn yourself in. I'm giving you one last chance to make me just a little bit proud of you. Maybe *then* we can talk. But not before."

"Please, you don't know what's coming."

I cut in and pointed off my property. "Do what I say, Jason!"

A silent stare-down followed, so strained you could pluck it like a guitar string.

Jason finally nodded as if in resignation. "Okay. I'll go. But promise me one thing. Be careful, Dad."

When I didn't answer, he turned and walked down the flagstone path to the gate in the hedge. He disappeared in the darkness of the alley. An engine started, and a car I never saw drove away.

I marched into the house, slammed the kitchen door, and leaned my back against it, my heart pounding. Had all this really happened, or had I only dreamed it?

I grabbed my phone out of my pocket and pulled up Wade's number. Jason had driven south. I should have checked what kind of car he was driving.

My thumb hovered over hitting the call button.

The fact was, I *hadn't* checked what kind of car Jason was driving. On purpose. I wanted my son to do the right thing for once. On his own. I wanted him to redeem himself. To give me at least one miserably small reason to be proud of him.

But I knew he never would.

I let the phone drop to my side. More than anything, I wanted my strapping young man back. My son.

I wiped the image of that idyllic past out of my mind. I never had a son.

Which meant I never had a granddaughter, either. Thank God.

Isolation was an addictively soothing drug.

# CHAPTER FIFTY
## JASON

He gripped the steering wheel with both hands, his knuckles white, and drove aimlessly. It could not have gone worse—his meeting with his dad. His mother's silver charm hadn't helped him at all. He and his dad were destined to ram against each other like a ship's bow being dashed by the waves. What had he accomplished tonight? Nothing. Except to learn that his father hated him more than he'd feared.

And that he had a daughter.

Jason tried and failed to wrap his mind around that idea. Could it really be true? Had he and Kalli brought a child into the world together? Not together. Jason had hit up his girlfriend, then skipped town. A sick, sinking feeling oozed through his chest. He hadn't even known. The girl was sixteen years old, and he hadn't even known she existed. Now Kalli was dead, and he was the only parent she had left. But he could never be there for her. He was on the run—now more than ever.

He found himself pulling up outside a restaurant. It was still open. It was risky to show his face in public. He shouldn't go in. But he needed to strategize, and he could do that better over a pot of coffee. Or a beer. But he was leaning toward the coffee. He needed to stay alert. He'd been up now for almost forty hours, and there was still no rest in sight.

He had a big decision to make. Leave Lake Geneva now, a free man ... or turn himself in to save countless lives. He kept wracking his brains for a third option, but it wasn't coming to him.

He parked and walked into the restaurant.

## CHAPTER FIFTY-ONE
## BAILEY

A guy walked in and took a booth. I grabbed an ice water and a menu and walked up to his table. "Hi, can I get you anything to drink?"

The guy looked up at me and said nothing. Just stared, like I'd asked the question in Greek. He shook his head as if clearing cobwebs. "Coffee," he finally said.

I rushed off to fill a pot and grab a mug, wondering if this guy planned on staring at me all night. He was probably going to camp out at his table until we started flicking out the lights as a not-so-subtle hint for him to pay his bill already and leave.

I set the mug in front of him, poured the coffee, and pulled my pad out of my apron pocket. "Ready to order?"

He asked for soup and a beef sandwich—staring at me the whole time.

"Do you work on the Mailboat?" he suddenly asked.

I smiled and nodded. "Yep."

"Your name's Bailey, right?"

"That's right. You've been on the Mailboat tour?"

He smiled. "Many times."

I liked his smile. Devilishly handsome, but a little sad. Perfect guy to play the tragic hero in a heart-wrenching movie.

"How long have you been jumping mail?" he asked me.

"This is my second year."

"I'll bet you're the best jumper on the crew."

I laughed. "Nah. I fell in just the other day."

"What grade are you in?"

"I'll be a junior."

"You like school?"

I nodded. "I love studying."

"What do you plan to do after graduation?"

I shrugged. "I'd like to go to college." Emphasis on *would like to*. After I turned eighteen, the foster care system would be done with me. Bud—if he was still my dad by then—wouldn't have a paying reason to keep me anymore. The reality was that my eighteenth birthday would find me on the street. Or the sole and permanent member of Bud's harem.

I would prefer to be on the street.

"What do you want to study?" the guy asked.

"Anything." Anything but how to find food in dumpsters.

He smiled. "You just like studying."

I nodded.

"You saving up those tips for college?"

I nodded again.

"You'll probably turn out to be a doctor or a lawyer."

I smiled. I knew I wanted my life to magically turn into a success, but I'd never seriously considered that I—Bailey Johnson—could make it *that* good. I envisioned a three-story house with a four-stall garage, and kinda liked it. LOL. And to think, I'd been picturing myself eating out of dumpsters a minute ago.

I wondered which future was more likely.

The guy motioned toward my face. "What happened to your eye?"

The cars I'd just been lining up in my garage vanished like air out of a flat tire. Seriously? Why did this have to keep coming up?

"I ran into something," I said.

"You ran into something, or something ran into you?"

"It happened when I fell off the Mailboat."

The man stared at me as if weighing my answer. "That must have hurt," he finally said.

I laughed it off and told him I'd better go hand his order in to the kitchen.

The rest of the night, his eyes followed me every time I walked into the dining room. He didn't finish his sandwich, but lingered a long time over the pot of coffee. Once, I found him leaning on his elbows with his face in his hands.

I stopped later and asked if he wanted more coffee. He said no. He studied my bruise again, then looked me deeply in the eyes, as if we were the only two people left in the universe.

"Few people in this world are truly alone," he said. "It's just a matter of finding the courage to reach out to someone when you need help."

O-o-okay. Didn't have a clue what brought that up.

"Bailey!" It was the cook yelling my name from the kitchen.

"Um—" I pointed over my shoulder. "I have to pick up an order."

He just nodded without taking his eyes off me.

When I came back into the dining room, the man was gone. I dropped off my other order, then went to clear his table. When I lifted the coffee cup, I found a folded bill underneath. The number in the corner stared up at me. One, zero, zero.

A hundred dollars? I looked up, but the man wasn't anywhere in the dining room. He must have made a mistake. I grabbed the bill and ran out the door to the parking lot. In the darkness, I spotted him on the far side of the lot, moving toward his car. I started down the sidewalk.

Out of the tree row on the edge of the lot, two men appeared. I made one out by the glints of light reflecting off silver studs in his jacket, and the other by the light shining off his completely bald head. They stepped up to the man I'd waited on and exchanged a few words I couldn't hear. My customer backed off slightly and raised his hands at the elbow. The big guy with the silver studs jerked his head toward another car, and the three walked in that direction. Studs and my customer got in the back seat while the bowling ball guy took the wheel. The engine started, and they drove off.

Okay, that was weird.

I looked down at the hundred dollar bill in my hand and tried to make sense out of what I'd just seen. It looked kinda like a kidnapping out of a movie. Was it? I mean, that sort of stuff just happened in the movies, right? Not in Lake Geneva. Then again, murders didn't happen in Lake Geneva, and Bailey Johnson certainly never found the body.

Maybe Bud would know what to do.

I walked into the bar. Rita was serving the drinks. Tonight, she was wearing a shirt so thin, I could see the color of her bra through the fabric. It was black. "Where's Bud?" I asked.

She jerked her head. "Having a smoke."

I went through the kitchen to the back door. An upside-down five-gallon bucket sat there, with a coffee can full of sand beside it.

No Bud.

# CHAPTER FIFTY-TWO
## MONICA

I sat on the floor in the dry storage room, my back against the wall, a cardboard box sitting beside me, and sheets of paper scattered across the floor. I massaged the corners of my eyes to keep them moist and open. I'd lost track of how long I'd been awake now. Twenty hours? Twenty-one?

The door opened and a pair of lean black slacks and matching shoes appeared. "I thought you were still around here somewhere," Wade said.

"Just going over the Bobby Markham files again," I said.

"Go home, Monica."

"In a minute."

"I can't afford to pay you any more overtime. Take tomorrow off."

"Not until we find Hart and Thomlin."

"Monica." The tone of his voice was stern. "Look, I know you're a go-getter, but you need to sleep. Are you even finding anything?"

I slapped my stack of papers down on the floor. "No." I massaged my eyes again. "I thought I had this all figured out, Wade, but none of this makes any sense. First I thought Jason was cleaning house so no one could spill his secrets and send him to jail. Now it looks as if Hart is trying to win Markham's affection by killing the men who supposedly led his son astray. But if that's the case, why did Fritz and Jason come back to Lake Geneva?"

"Maybe Hart lured them back somehow."

"With what?"

"Sleep on it. It'll make sense in the morning."

I gave him a tired smile. "Promise?"

"Yes, I promise."

"Fine. I'm going home."

"You have a long drive."

"Just to Fontana." Twenty minutes via South Lake Shore Drive. It wasn't far, by my reckoning. But I was used to it.

"Whatever. I don't want to see you here tomorrow."

"Yes, Chief." I threw the papers back into the box and stood up.

"Promise?" he asked.

"Promise," I replied.

## CHAPTER FIFTY-THREE
## RYAN

I truly was a loser.

My sergeant had given me my day shift off, due to the shooting. Not because I'd done anything wrong or because of the investigation or all that. Just because my ribs hurt like heck and he felt sorry for me. I slept past noon.

Then I volunteered for night shift again when I heard that the guy I had been filling in for was still sick.

Hence I was a loser.

I had no desire to patrol the area where I'd been shot at the night before. Aside from the fact that I'd been transformed into a giant black-and-blue mark on legs, I was okay. But just the thought of what had happened—and what could have happened—made my stomach churn.

I made myself drive down Main Street anyway. Just to show myself I was tougher than some old man with a Ferrari and a gun.

## CHAPTER FIFTY-FOUR
## JASON

With both Charles and his henchman training their guns on him, Jason had no choice but to get into their car. He slid into the back seat and moved over to the far side while the big guy with the leather vest and tattoos joined him. In a million years, Jason never would have pictured Charles keeping company with someone like that.

But he'd never pictured any of this happening at all.

Fritz dead. Himself as good as dead. It was only the beginning of the bloodbath that only he knew about. And his dad was deaf to hearing a single word of it. He'd failed in every way.

Including as a father.

Bailey's face sat in the center of his mind. She'd inherited his wavy brown hair, but she had her mother's eyes and delicate little nose. He'd known in a heartbeat that the girl in the bar was his and Kalli's.

His heart cracked. If not for the burly, leather-clad thug sitting beside him, he would have buried his face in his hands and bawled like a child. The girl was a little piece of Kalli, and he could never have her. Even if he survived tonight. His past would run him to ground.

How had he failed so miserably at life?

Maybe his dad was right. He should turn himself in. At least that way, Bailey could come visit him in prison.

Through a glass wall. Over a phone.

It wasn't the same.

Jason eyed the Glock, resting on the man's beefy thigh. In the very near future—as soon as they got wherever they were going—that Glock would be pointed at Jason's head, and it would all be over. The question was ... Was he ready to die tonight? Was he calling it quits?

He set his jaw. No. He wasn't. Tonight was not his night to die.

He reached for the gun to wrench it from the thug's hand.

"Hey!" The man's finger slipped over the trigger.

*Boom.*

Jason's ears rang with the explosion in the small space. The car swerved, tipping sideways as two wheels left the road.

*Crack.*

Metal ripped. Glass exploded. The car stopped so fast Jason was vaulted out of his seat, into the back of the front passenger seat. Airbags popped open.

Everything was suddenly stock still and dead quiet, except for the tinkle of glass dropping and the hiss of something leaking in the engine.

Jason groaned and hugged his ribs. Lifting his face from the back of the chair in front of him, he blinked at a young birch tree sitting in the passenger seat.

He'd come *that* close to head-butting a tree at thirty-five miles per hour.

The guy in the leather vest groaned and stirred.

Jason's heart leapt. Where was the gun? Where was the gun? The man's hands were empty. He felt around the back seat in the dark. Then the floor. Where was it?

He looked into the front seat and saw it sitting on the console. He grabbed it.

Just as he did, a click sounded in his ear. He turned slowly, into the nose of a tidy little Remington revolver in Charles's hand.

Memories frolicked at the edge of Jason's mind. Three boys. Running up and down marble halls. Hiding under a table. Waiting for Charles to pass by. Tucking daisies into the laces of his shoes. Giggling.

Jason looked into the face of an old man with a stream of blood running down the side of his face and nothing but murder in his eyes.

He struck the gun away and dove into the back seat. The Remington got off a bullet that went wild. Jason grabbed the door latch and pushed against the door.

Jammed.

With a roar, thick arms clamped around Jason's neck from behind and dragged him back. Jason grabbed the arm with his free hand and tried to pull it loose enough for him to breathe, but the man was built like a bear.

All was fair in love and war. Jason reached back over his head and felt for the man's eyes. When he heard a scream and felt the choke arm go loose, he knew he'd struck home. He tucked his chin in, lifted his shoulders, and slipped through the vice. Using the Glock, he smashed open the window and dove through, head-first, landing in broken glass.

He got up immediately and ran. The stretch of road was desolate. No driveways on either side. No houses. Just trees. His ribs ached. Blood ran down his hand. His knee was killing him. He should have joined the baseball team like his dad said. He should have done a lot of things like his dad said.

Car doors rattled and burst open.

"Stop!"

No way.

*Bang.*

Jason yelled and pitched forward. Everything came to a halt as he landed face-first on asphalt. Searing hot pain flashed through his back and chest.

No.

No, no, no.

An image of a young girl with wavy brown hair blinked across his eyes. So sweet. So much like Kalli. His dad said someone was abusing her.

Jason groaned and pushed himself to his knees. He'd find a house. Call an ambulance. Turn himself in. Spend the rest of his life in prison. Visit his daughter through glass over a phone.

*Bang.*

Jason dropped again with another scream. This one gurgled and sputtered. He felt like he was drowning. He coughed, a horrible, phlegmy cough, and his mouth filled with the taste of blood.

He squeezed his eyes shut as tears rolled down his face. *Dad, why wouldn't you listen?*

Footsteps drew near behind him, crunching slowly on the stones on the road.

Jason tightened his grip on the Glock but couldn't pull together the strength to roll over and face his killers.

A pair of shining black Oxfords stopped right in front of Jason's nose. The Remington clicked.

In his mind, Jason tucked a pair of daisies into the laces.

## CHAPTER FIFTY-FIVE
## BAILEY

I jumped into Bud's car and gripped the steering wheel, waves of guilt flooding over me. I knew how to drive a car. I just didn't have my license yet.

If I was wrong ... and if Bud found out ... I was toast. But my gut and my mind were screaming opposite things.

I wrenched the key in the ignition and jabbed the headlights on. Backing out of the parking space was the hard part. I nearly left a dent in the dumpster. After that, I found my way to South Lake Shore Drive—the direction I thought they took—and was home free.

I didn't have a clue how exactly I expected to find them in the dark after such a long delay. They could have turned off anywhere by now. But just as loudly as my gut had screamed to follow them, my gut was screaming now to just stick to the same road.

Who was the guy in the diner? Why had he been so interested in me and left me that hundred-dollar bill? Why had he gotten into that car with those other men? Why had he—?

I rounded a corner and slammed the brakes, a scream jumping out of my mouth.

My headlights picked out a man lying flat in the middle of my lane. Another man stood over him, pointing down at him.

No. Pointing a *gun* down at him.

My tires screeched as I skidded across the asphalt. I jumped on the brake with both feet and all my weight. How long did it take to make a car *stop?* I was only driving thirty-five miles an hour!

Okay, forty.

I finally jolted to a halt mere yards in front of the two men. The one lying in the road was barely visible over the hood. I saw the wavy brown-and-gray hair on the back of his head.

The guy from the diner.

A car sat ahead of me in the ditch, its hood crumpled against a tree. A big guy stood near an open rear door, dressed in a black leather vest with silver studs.

*Boom.*

I screamed and ducked sideways as spiderweb cracks radiated from a hole in my windshield.

The guy with the bowling ball head was shooting. At me. I'd just interrupted a murder in progress.

I was so toast.

And now Bud would know I'd borrowed his car. No good alibis sprang to mind to explain a bullet hole in the windshield.

Another gunshot exploded, sending my heart into my throat. What should I do?

A crazy thought popped into my head. If Bud could fit under this car on a creeper ...

I sprang back up into a sitting position and hit the gas. The tires squealed before the car jumped forward like a race horse out of the starting gate.

An expression of shock flashed across the man's face.

He was an old man, with wrinkles around clear blue eyes. A stream of blood ran down one side of his face.

My stomach flipped. What the heck was I doing? I pulled my foot off the gas, but I was already flying.

The old man lunged sideways. The car sailed over the guy on the ground without so much as a bump. I stomped on the brake again and jolted to a stop a car's length beyond his prone body.

I looked back over my shoulder in time to see the old man raise his gun while walking toward me swiftly.

Okay, I shouldn't have been nice.

I couldn't back into him. Images of nearly denting the dumpster sprang to mind. I'd squash the guy on the ground if I tried the same tactic in reverse. Nothing for it but to run—maybe turn around in a driveway. I couldn't leave the poor guy they were trying to kill. I whipped around in my seat to face the windshield again, swearing I'd practice my reverse driving when this was over.

Before I so much as touched the gas pedal, another shot went off. A second hole ruptured in my windshield. The guy in the leather vest had a gun, too.

*Squish him,* daring Bailey urged.

*I don't know how,* normal Bailey countered.

I mean, technically, I knew how. Apply the gas and point the steering wheel in his direction. What I didn't know how to do was kill another human being. Like the dead body at the end of the pier. Like the dead-or-alive guy in the middle of the road. I didn't even know who any of these people were. How I'd gotten tangled up in this mess. All I knew was that I didn't have whatever it takes to suck a living soul out of a body and leave the carcass behind. I'd rather die along with the other guy.

I was hemmed in. The man in leather in front of me, the old man behind me to my right, their victim somewhere beyond my rear bumper. More gunshots went off. All of them aimed at me.

I screamed.

# CHAPTER FIFTY-SIX
## RYAN

My radio crackled. "LGPD to all units. Caller reports shots fired."

Fear shot up my spine. I wasn't exactly eager to encounter gunfire again. Maybe this time, it was just somebody shooting fireworks prematurely. I hoped so.

The address the dispatcher gave was on South Lake Shore Drive. The two other units on patrol tonight radioed in their availability. I took a deep breath, getting ready to report mine.

The vest I was wearing tonight was an ill-fitting spare that had been sitting in storage at the station. I was just using it until the new one ordered for me came in. But Kevlar was Kevlar, and the stuff had saved my life once. I thumped my chest to re-assure myself. I was coming home tonight. I wasn't ready for an obituary yet. I had to do something worth obituating about first.

I clicked the button on my mic. "Forty-four thirty-seven to LGPD, ten-four. ETA, five minutes."

I flipped on the lights. I was ready. But this was definitely the last time I ever filled in for another guy.

## CHAPTER FIFTY-SEVEN
## MONICA

I had my radio scanner turned on as I drove home and heard the shots fired call. I also heard 4437 respond. Brandt. What the hell was he doing on patrol again tonight?

I'd already passed the address. I glanced both ways, made a U-turn, and hit the gas. I had a spare gun in my glove box and was still wearing my vest under my polo shirt. I didn't have a radio mic, though. Instead, I pulled out my cell phone and called the station. No one picked up. I assumed the dispatcher was still on the line with the caller. There wouldn't be a second dispatcher this time of night.

I sighed and hung up. I didn't want to show up at this situation without *somebody* knowing I was coming.

I tapped my fingers on the steering wheel, then grabbed my phone again. I pressed Brandt's name in my contacts.

Funny I still had him in there.

"Hello?"

"Brandt? It's Monica. I heard the call on my scanner. I'm on my way. I'll be approaching from the south."

Silence. "Okay."

Okay? What did *okay* mean? More importantly, what did the silence mean? I sighed in frustration. "See you in five," I said.

I was just about to hang up when he spoke again. "Monica?"

"What?"

"Be careful."

Now it was my turn to play the crickets track. There was something sweet about him telling me to watch my back.

I shoved the thought aside. "See you in five," I said again.

## CHAPTER FIFTY-EIGHT
## BAILEY

*Bang.*

The right rear window shattered.

I popped open the door and rolled out onto the pavement. The scream that pierced the air was my own.

*Bang. Bang. Bang.*

My initial plan had been to run. But as the mood of the evening took on a Fourth-of-July feel, I tucked into a ball and laced my fingers over my head. I was toast. This was it. The end to Bailey Johnson's sad existence. I'd be all over the newspapers and people would say, "Gees, that loser? Why'd anybody bother to murder her?" At least I'd have no next-of-kin to trouble with my pitiful demise.

But when I failed to feel any bullets ripping me into confetti, I dared to peek.

My jaw dropped. The guy on the ground had come back to life. Propped on one elbow, he squeezed off bullets in the direction of the old man and the guy in leather.

Flashes of light popped in the darkness. Over and over and over. Back and forth. Back and forth. Until a scream ripped the air, sending chills up my spine. My stomach churned. Somebody'd been hit. The only person I could see was the man on the ground, and he was still firing bullets.

A body hurdled over the top of me—and before I knew what was happening, the guy in the vest had jumped over me and slammed the door shut on Bud's car. The tires screeched beside my ear. I slid sideways to get out of the way—then rolled back the other direction as the driver made a U-turn and came back at me. But instead of running me over, he shot into the darkness and out of sight.

Crap. I'd just gotten Bud's car stolen.

All of a sudden, South Lake Shore Drive was eerily quiet. Like a graveyard after all the ghosts are done flying around and screaming and have gone back to their tombs, and you wonder if anything really happened at all. I slowly got up, shaking, and hugged myself as I sat on my heels and looked around.

The old man lay motionless, sprawled on his back. The man with the wavy hair had collapsed again. He was making a horrible, wet coughing sound.

I clamped my teeth and eyes shut as my stomach churned. I rocked myself, feeling cold and alone and terrified. Hot tears ran down my cheeks. This was the worst night of my life. Ever. And I randomly just wanted somebody to show up and hold me close and make it all go away.

But no one was here. It was just me. And two guys were lying on the ground next to me, dead or dying. One of them had left me a hundred-dollar bill under a plate a few minutes ago.

I wiped the tears out of my eyes and pushed myself up onto wobbly legs. Rubbing my arms, I staggered over to where he lay gasping and coughing. I choked down my fear and knelt beside him.

He turned cloudy brown eyes up at me. A furrow flickered between his brows. "Bailey?"

No doubt the waitress from the restaurant was the last person he'd expected to see.

"Yeah," I said. "You tipped too much."

He made a noise which I think was intended to be a laugh but came out instead as a cough. Blood sputtered out of his mouth.

I grabbed my cell phone out of my back pocket. "You better lie still. I'll call an ambulance."

He shook his head. "Mmmet the gun." His words were garbled.

"What?"

"The gun."

I pointed to the one he still held in his hand. "This one?"

"No. The gun."

He looked frantic. I scrambled to think which gun, and finally realized he wanted the other guy's weapon. Great. I had to go over there?

"Hurry."

I got up on wobbly legs and staggered over to the man with the bowling ball head. My stomach flipped and I almost chucked up the dinner I'd had an hour ago. There was a hole smack in the middle of his forehead. A hole. Blood covered the ground under his head.

Forcing myself not to look at the carnage, I grabbed the gun out of his limp hand. Just like I'd grabbed a knife out of another dead man's hand. This was shaping up to be the worst summer ever. I limped back to my customer and dropped beside him, still crying. I showed him the gun.

"Is he dead?"

"Yeah."

"You sure?"

I nodded. Heck, yeah, I was sure.

The man sighed—and started coughing again.

"I'll call an ambulance." I pulled my phone out of my pocket again.

He grabbed my hand, stopping me before I could even unlock the screen. "Bailey," he said.

I waited for him to say something more, but he simply stared up at me, chest heaving.

"Let me call an ambulance," I said.

"Too late."

"Shut up."

I wrenched my hand free and slid the lock across the screen.

The man scowled ferociously and reached up to his neck. He grabbed at the collar of his tee shirt frantically, as if searching for something.

"What are you doing?"

His fist closed over something and he ripped it away from his chest with a jerk. Something snapped, and two ends of a fine ball chain dangled from his fist. He grabbed my hand, knocking my phone to the pavement, and jammed whatever-it-was into my palm.

"What is it?"

He closed my fingers over it tightly. "Keep it," he whispered.

"Okay, fine. I'll keep it."

One hand still closed around mine, he stared up at me. His eyes began to glisten and a fat tear rolled down his cheek.

I didn't get any of this. "Can I call the ambulance now?"

"Whatever you want, Princess."

My gut twisted in a hundred soul-crushing knots. Had he just called me *Princess?* Nobody had ever called me that before. I'd never so much as wanted anybody to call me that, because I'd never remotely imagined anybody ever would. Now that I heard it, it sounded distinctly like the kind of thing a dad might call his little girl.

I suddenly wanted to smash this guy's face in. Who did he think he was, calling me by a name only my dad had any right to call me?

Then again, *what* dad? I'd never had one. Probably never would—unless this guy really was a lonely, childless millionaire.

His hand on mine loosened and slid down. His breathing became shallow and sporadic.

My heart pounded. "Mister? Hey, no, don't go anywhere."

I dropped his hand and fumbled for my phone. But by the time I'd found it and turned on the screen, his face had changed. His eyes were half shut. His gaze frozen. As if he were staring at something in a different world.

"No, no, no!" I grabbed his shoulders and shook him. My whole body trembled, even my voice. "Please don't. Don't die."

No answer.

Tears spilled over my cheeks. He was gone. I faintly heard the patter of my own feet fade and vanish down a marble hall.

Apparently, if I so much as dreamed of a dad of my own, the guy was as good as dead. I felt as if I'd just killed him myself.

Scalding tears streamed down my face.

Not for him.

For me. All I wanted was a dad. Was that such a horrible thing to ask for?

I heard sirens in the distance. Somebody must have heard the gunshots. Seriously, how could anybody miss them? The police would be on the way—but too late. It was over.

Everything was over.

But no one was here to see. Not yet. Neither was there anybody else around to mourn this guy's death. And I couldn't kill him any deader than he already was.

I slowly leaned down and laid my head on his chest. My throat squeezed so tight, I could hardly breathe. Something inside me screamed like a baby—a baby with a double-quadruple earache—but not a peep escaped my mouth. I was screaming for a daddy—or *anybody*—to give half a damn about me. And all I had was a dead man.

I closed my eyes and cried. He felt warm. That didn't help any. The tears came in tsunamis. I cried like I'd never cried in my life, for what felt like a century, until I didn't have a tear left.

Lights careened around the corner. Yellow headlights. Red and blue emergency lights. The cops were here.

I lifted my head and blinked down at my dreamed-of dad until the blur faded. He looked peaceful. I felt like crap. I sat up and dried my eyes on my sleeve.

Doors popped open and men jumped out of cars. Another car without the red and blue lights came from the other direction and screeched to a stop.

"Police! Put your hands up!"

What were they talking about? Everybody was dead.

"Put your hands up! Put your hands up!"

I suddenly realized they were talking to me. They wanted me to put my hands up. Did they think I'd killed both these guys?

My hand was still closed around whatever it was that the dead man had pressed into my palm. I ignored the voices screaming at me and opened my fingers.

A silver ship's wheel on a tarnished ball chain.

Another voice called more softly. "Bailey?"

I knew that voice. Whose voice was that? It didn't matter. It wasn't the one voice I would have liked to hear most at that moment. It wasn't Tommy's.

"Bailey, it's Ryan. Honey, we need you to put your hands up."

I laced the chain around my fingers and raised my hands.

They made me stand up and walk toward them backwards.

They handcuffed me.

It was just protocol, Ryan said in my ear. It was for everyone's safety. He said it just before he touched me all over. My head told me he was looking for weapons. The

209

screaming little girl inside me screamed all the louder. Fresh tears spilled down my cheeks. I didn't want to be touched.

A figure appeared out of the blinding headlights of one of the cars. She was tall and thin with long, dark hair tied back in a ponytail. "They're both dead," she said to Ryan. "It's Jason and Charles."

Ryan swore. Then he sighed and looked at me, his eyes hurting. "Bailey, what happened here?"

I squeezed my eyes shut again and held on tightly to the ship's wheel.

## CHAPTER FIFTY-NINE
## BUD

Bud maneuvered the turns of South Lake Shore Drive at about sixty while trying to dial up a number on his phone. The lights of the street lamps reflected off the bullet holes in his windshield, making it hard to see. What the hell had Bailey been doing driving his car?

Paying little heed to lanes, he nearly plowed head-first into an oncoming car. He swerved, ignored the blaring horn, and kept driving. He had to dump this car somewhere and run back to the bar before anyone knew he was missing. But had Bailey recognized him?

He finally got the number typed in and hit send. It wasn't the kind of number you kept in your contacts. Or your call history. Or your head, if you could avoid it. But Bud wasn't the type to avoid this kind of number. He had to talk to The Man—or The Man Upstairs, as he liked to call him. What the hell, the guy thought he was God.

The line rang four times.

"C'mon, pick up," Bud muttered.

The line clicked. "What are you doing, calling me?"

"He's dead," Bud replied, swerving around another corner. The realization was finally sinking in. He started to shake. He'd seen a hole ripped straight through Charles's head.

"Jason?"

"No. Yes. I mean Charles. He took my gun and shot him."

"Slow down, man. You're not making any sense."

Sweat from his brow was running into his eyes. He didn't have a free hand to wipe it away. He rubbed his face on his sleeve. "Jason disarmed me and shot Charles. Charles is dead."

Silence engulfed the line.

"So Jason got away?" The Man finally asked.

"No. He's dead, too."

"Oh, good." There was a pause, but not long enough. "It's a pity about Charles. Never mind, though. The plan will go on."

"What the hell are you talking about?" Didn't this dude have a piteous bone in his body?

"The plan. Will. Go on. Now then. I suggest you get back to your bar before anyone misses you."

"Someone already did."

The man's voice took on a hard tone. "What do you mean?"

"Bailey. My foster kid. She followed me."

The Man Upstairs cussed under his breath. "Did she see you?"

"Yes, but I don't think she recognized me."

"Find out if she did. We may have to deal with her."

Bud gaped at his phone. "What are you talkin' about, deal with Bailey?"

"Bud." The tone of his voice left no room for argument. "The plan. Must. Go on."

## THANK YOU

Dear Reader,

Thank you so much for picking up *Mailboat: Book One*, the first in a mystery series set in Lake Geneva, Wisconsin. I hope you enjoyed it and want to find out what happens to Bailey, Tommy, Ryan, and Monica! (There's a sneak peek at Book Two in just a few pages.)

Would your curiosity be piqued if I told you there was a way for you to support me and all your favorite authors, beyond the price of the book you're reading—and that it wouldn't cost you a penny?

**Why not leave a review at your favorite online bookstore!**

Readers won't buy a book with few reviews, but it's hard to ignore a book sporting lots of four- and five-star recommendations!

So if you like what you just read and wanna see some more, why not support an author by letting the world know what you thought of this book?

Thanks, and happy reading!

Danielle Lincoln Hanna

## ABOUT THE MAILBOAT
## AND LAKE GENEVA, WISCONSIN

*A Note from the Author*

I didn't realize Wrigley Drive was a one-way until I got there. I ended up going around the block to start again from the right end. Once or twice a week—okay, maybe more than that—I have what I call "a Bailey moment," and this was one of them.

It was six o'clock on a Saturday morning, August 9th, 2014. My dog, a German Shepherd/Rottweiler named Molly, stood at attention on the back seat. You'd think after two days on the road, she'd finally lie down, but no. She was almost as excited as I was. We were finally in Lake Geneva, Wisconsin.

I turned the corner onto Wrigley Drive and the lake came into full view, framed in the foreground by the trees in Library Park, and in the background by hills that rolled down to meet the water. The sun was just rising, tinting both the sky and the water a delicate pink.

"Oh my God, it's real," I said. The words slipped out of my mouth before I even knew what I was saying.

It was even more beautiful than everything I'd seen in photos and videos. Beyond that, I had the strangest feeling.

Not as if I were exploring some place I'd never been before, but as if I were coming home.

The next moment, the Riviera came into view, and the piers behind it, and right there ...

The Mailboat.

"Oh my God, it's real," I said again.

Up until now, the Mailboat—and Lake Geneva itself—had existed in my mind as the setting for a mystery novel. While I knew it was a real place and a real boat, they had been tinted with a layer of fictionalization. Now, to actually see the place for myself became surreal, as if I'd somehow dropped through the pages of my book and landed in the story.

Bailey, Captain Tommy, Ryan, and Monica are works of fiction, as are the events in the series, but Lake Geneva, Wisconsin, and the Mailboat are not. Every summer, high school and college kids carry on the tradition of jumping mail from boat to pier around the 21-mile perimeter of the lake. And I was here to see it for myself.

After driving past the Mailboat—just to take a quick peek—I wove my way into the heart of the town to find Molly's doggy daycare. My route took me past turn-of-the-century houses with front porches and gingerbread trim and pristine lawns shaded by old trees.

These houses were tiny compared to what I was about to see on the lake itself. Lake Geneva, Wisconsin, is a hidden gem of the Midwest. The railroad line from Chicago to the lake was completed about the same time that the Chicago Fire decimated the city. Many of Chicago's business barons moved to the lake while their homes were being rebuilt, then made a tradition of returning every summer. The shoreline has changed dramatically over the years, but Geneva Lake (as the body of water is known) is still the playground of millionaires, ringed by stunning mansions.

I got Molly settled into her daycare, then turned around to go back to the Mailboat. The managers had agreed to let me job shadow the captain and crew for a couple of days as research for the series. I had butterflies in my stomach. I had a back-stage pass to one of Lake Geneva's most treasured icons.

In the early days, all transportation to the lakeside estates was conducted by boat, since there were no good roads. Even the mail was delivered by boat—and thus a tradition was begun. Official Mailboat delivery was established in 1916. Today, the Walworth II carries on that tradition, for nostalgia's sake. The tour includes both the daring mail deliveries, as well as a narrated tour of the history of the homes around the lake, with names like Wrigley, Maytag, and Schwinn cropping up around every bend in the shore.

I found a place to park my car and walked through Library Park, my heart pounding. I could barely convince myself that all this was real. For a moment, I was Bailey, walking to work on a Saturday morning. I strolled under the archways of the Riviera and down the wooden pier. During my first day on the Mailboat, it felt like a place I'd been thousands of times. I spent the rest of the morning following the mail jumpers and the captain.

I was back again the next day, and one more day after that. On my third day, they let me try mail jumping myself. I almost wound up frozen on the pier, too afraid to throw myself at the boat as it sailed past. But I made it. The things I'll do for research. (You can see a video at www.DanielleLincolnHanna.com/my-stint-as-a-lake-geneva-mail-jumper/.)

Since then, I've been on the Mailboat tour several times—usually with a notepad and pen in hand—and I would not hesitate to say, this is something you need to do at least once in your life: Take the Mailboat cruise.

The tour runs from June 15th through September 15th every summer. Mail is delivered Monday through Saturday, with newspaper deliveries on Sunday. Tickets are available through the Lake Geneva Cruise Line. You can check them out at www.CruiseLakeGeneva.com. I hope you do!

Meanwhile, I have more mysteries to write about a certain young mail jumper ...

## CHAPTER ONE
## TOMMY

I woke up the next morning with a stellar headache, my argument with my son rolling through my head. For one of the few times in forty-eight years, I considered calling in sick. But it took more than that for me to miss a Mailboat run. Not even the morning after my son robbed a bank, killed a cop, and skipped town. I drove the Mailboat that day. Just as always.

The day my son abandoned his mother and me. And his daughter.

My stomach roiled. Bailey was my granddaughter. I didn't have the option of sitting on the sidelines anymore. Some brute was laying hands on my granddaughter and sending her off to me every morning with welts and bruises. If I'd despised him before, I despised him doubly now.

There was no question about stepping in for Bailey. Ending the abuse. Making sure she was safe. That much, I could do, and I would.

But then what? Was I ready to go beyond that point and be her grandfather?

I closed my eyes and rubbed my aching forehead.

1

No.

The answer was no.

I skipped breakfast and grabbed my keys. I wouldn't tell Bailey. Not yet. Maybe not ever. I could help her without having to get too involved. Without her ever having to know.

A knock sounded on the front door.

The sun was barely over the horizon. My mind scrambled for a moment to think who would be up as early as me. Generally speaking, Wade was the only one who ever walked up to my door.

Dear God, he was right. I was isolated.

I glanced out the bow window in the living room, and sure enough, Wade stood on the porch. In uniform.

The first thought through my mind was that something had happened to Bailey. Why else would he be here so early? I threw back the lock and opened the door.

"Tommy."

"Wade. What is it? I was just leaving for work."

Wade chewed his lip. "I think you'd better call in."

"Why? Is this about Bailey?"

Wade shook his head.

Relief washed over me. "Then what's this about?"

Wade worked his jaw before making his one-word reply. "Jason."

The bottom dropped out of my heart and whatever was inside hit the deck. They'd caught him. Or had he actually turned himself in? Either way, he was arrested. Seventeen long years of waiting was over.

I shut my eyes momentarily, letting the cold, hard reality sink in. "You arrested him?" I finally asked.

To my surprise, Wade shook his head.

For a fleeting moment, I entertained the fantasy that it had all been some unfathomable mistake. That Jason was innocent. Of everything. I envisioned a table set with mounds of humble pie, and me savoring every bite.

2

"He's dead, Tommy."

I stared.

"Do you want me to call Robb?" Wade asked.

I didn't reply. The words were still sinking in. "How can he be dead?" I finally asked.

"Come here, Tommy." Wade herded me toward the antique park bench on my front porch and made me sit. He sat next to me. Looked me in the eye. "Tommy, I so hate to tell you this. He was killed."

Killed? Someone had killed my son? I stared blankly across the street as my neighbor's sprinkler system sputtered to life. A minute dragged by. Two. I couldn't find words. Only feel a growing emptiness that gnawed on every tender part of my soul.

"We're still working out the details," Wade said. "But it looks as if he was kidnapped and ..." He stopped and worked his jaw again. "He died of gunshot wounds," he finished.

I'd seen him just last night. I'd spoken to him. I'd unleashed all my pent-up fury on him and sent him away. My last act as his father. I'd sent him away to his death.

I buried my face in my hands. "Dear God."

"I'll call Robb," Wade said softly.

I shook my head. "No."

"Tommy, you're not driving the Mailboat today."

I wanted to snap at him. I most certainly *was*. I wanted to be on the Mailboat this morning. I wanted everything to be normal. I wanted my son back. That's all I'd ever wanted. I just wanted my son back.

"You know I'd never ask you this unless I had to," Wade said. "But I need you to come with me this morning. I need you to give me a positive identification."

My eyes snapped to his. It wasn't positive?

At the look of hope on my face, Wade's eyes saddened. "For protocol, Tommy."

3

I stared at my friend, wishing there was some way to turn back the clock. Some way to return to those idyllic days when I had both Elaina and Jason and everything was happy. Now here I was, the last one left alive. Feeling as dead as I could possibly be.

"Tell me this isn't happening, Wade," I whispered.

Wade shook his head. "I wish I could."

. . .

*Want to know when Book Two is available? Make sure to join my newsletter!*

www.DanielleLincolnHanna.com/newsletter

## ACKNOWLEDGMENTS

If you've ever set foot in Lake Geneva, Wisconsin, you will not soon forget it. From the white-painted piers to the boutique shopping to—of course—the Mailboat itself, there is something about the place that residents describe as "beautiful," "peaceful," and "idyllic." Residents and vacationers alike love their little jewel in the trees. One girl I met even had an outline of the lake tattooed on her foot.

Setting a novel in a real location means no end of research. But setting a novel in a town as beloved as Lake Geneva, Wisconsin, came with its own responsibilities. I knew I had to "get it right." Any errors are, of course, my own, but anything I got right is largely thanks to a whole crew of Lake Geneva residents who helped me out.

To the management and staff of the Lake Geneva Cruise Line and the Lake Geneva Mailboat, thanks for letting me job shadow, hang around the boat, take the tour multiple times, and even try mail jumping. Thanks specifically to *General Managers Harold Friestad* and *Jack Lothian,* for facilitating me. *Captain Neill Frame, Captain Ray Ames,* and *mail jumpers Joanie Williams, Dan Sepe, Shelby Peck, Kylie McCarter,* and *Fiona McCarter* for letting me job shadow you and ask dozens of questions. Huge thanks goes to *Office Manager Ellen Burling* for being my contact person from start to finish and arranging everything, from my behind-the-scenes tours to the photography of the real Mailboat used on the cover art. Every time I asked, "So, do you think we can (fill in the blank)?" I expected you to finally slam the door in my face. Instead, you replied almost every time with, "Sure, we can do that." Ellen, you rock!

Many local residents also had a hand in helping me get to know the lake. Thank you to "Lake Geneva-ites" *W. J. Goes and M. Farewell Goes* for letting me meet you at your beautiful home and for the trip to the country club in your classic wooden boat. *Lynda Fergus,* I still use the coffee mug you gave me from The Coffee Mill! Thank you for the tour of Fontana. You're right, it was short. But I fell in love with it, and now Monica lives there. (Totally your fault.) *Jamie Ploch,* I'm so glad I decided to ask a librarian where to find an abandoned barn and other strange things for the series. You've been a huge help in my research ever since then.

While the Mailboat is central to the series, so is the Lake Geneva Police Department. Much gratitude to *Sgt. Jason Hall* for the tour of the police station, *Dispatcher Rita Moore* for the tour of her dispatch room, and *Officer Katie Teitz* for the ride along.

I also want to give a big shout out to my Early Reader Team: *Loranda Daniels Buoy, Lynda Fergus, Eleanor F.J. Gamarsh, Connie Hanna, Rebecca Paciorek, Jamie Ploch, Sanda Putnam,* and *Carol D. Westover.* Thank you for reviewing the manuscript and catching my errors! Thanks also for your words of enthusiasm about the book. I'm so glad you liked it!

A special thanks goes to the law enforcement professionals who reviewed my manuscript for accuracy: *Lt. Ed Gritzner* and *Sgt. Jason Hall* of the Lake Geneva Police Department and *Sam Petitto,* retired police officer, Durango, CO.

Also, thanks to *Matt Mason Photography* (www.MattMasonPhotography.com) for the photo of the Mailboat that became the front cover, *W. J. Goes* for escorting my photography crew around the lake in his Boston whaler, and *MaryDes* (www.MaryDes.eu) for the stellar cover design.

You guys have all been massively instrumental in the making of this book, and I thank you.

Oh, and thanks to my dog Molly. Cuz she wanted to be in the acknowledgments.

## JOIN MY NEWSLETTER!

- Be the *first* to know about all my new releases
- Access *exclusive* discounts, freebies, and contests
- Get *way* behind the scenes
- Even *help me* write my next book!

Just visit me at
www.DanielleLincolnHanna.com/newsletter

73282506R00143

Made in the USA
Lexington, KY
07 December 2017